CIRCLE

LOVER'S ABSOLUTION

Other books by R. A. Steffan

The Last Vampire: Book One
The Last Vampire: Book Two
The Last Vampire: Book Three
The Last Vampire: Book Four
The Last Vampire: Book Five
The Last Vampire: Book Six

Vampire Bound: Book One
Vampire Bound: Book Two
Vampire Bound: Book Three
Vampire Bound: Book Four

Forsaken Fae: Book One
Forsaken Fae: Book Two
Forsaken Fae: Book Three

The Sixth Demon: Book One
The Sixth Demon: Book Two
The Sixth Demon: Book Three

The Complete Horse Mistress Collection
The Complete Lion Mistress Collection
The Complete Dragon Mistress Collection
The Complete Master of Hounds Collection

Antidote: Love and War, Book 1
Antigen: Love and War, Book 2
Antibody: Love and War, Book 3
Anthelion: Love and War, Book 4
Antagonist: Love and War, Book 5

Circle of Blood Book Four:

Lover's Absolution

R. A. Steffan & Jaelynn Woolf

Circle of Blood Book Four: Lover's Absolution

Copyright 2018 by R. A. Steffan

This book is a work of fiction. Names, characters, businesses, organizations, places, events and incidents either are the product of the author's imagination or are used fictitiously. Any resemblance to actual persons, living or dead, events, or locales is entirely coincidental.

ISBN: 978-1-955073-43-1(paperback)

For information, contact the author at
http://www.rasteffan.com/contact/

Cover art by Deranged Doctor Design

Second Edition: December 2022

INTRODUCTION

This book contains graphic violence and explicit sexual content. It is intended for a mature audience. While it is part of a series with an over-arching plot, it can be read as a standalone with a "happy ever after" ending for the two main characters, and a satisfying resolution of the storyline. If you don't intend to continue the series, you may wish to avoid the epilogue.

TABLE OF CONTENTS

ONE

"Oh, you have *got* to be shitting me," Xander said, as a dozen werewolves appeared in the mouth of the dead-end London alley.

"Sorry," said the dark-haired woman who'd lured him here on the pretext of helping her—apparently fictional—sister who had supposedly been attacked by a young boy with glowing eyes and fangs. She sounded genuinely sheepish as she jerked her chin at the man next to her, who was decked out in chains and ripped camo like some sort of cut-rate Mad Max reject. "He didn't think you'd come if you knew what we really were, vampire."

"Smarter than he looks, then," Xander observed, thinking privately that it wasn't a very high bar to reach. "Good to know."

The alpha werewolf's answering smile was thin and cruel. "You'd be amazed." He cocked his head. "No doubt you're getting ready to fly away home, little vamp, but you should hear what I have to tell you first. I've got something you want."

"You think so?" Xander asked, affecting boredom to cover his irritation at having fallen for a pretty woman's damsel-in-distress act. "What is it? Fleas? Kibbles? A squeaky toy? Maybe a nice, meaty bone?"

That cruel smile never wavered. "I've got that little baby vamp Manisha described to you, all chained up in iron shackles, so he can't get away. Interested, now?"

Yes. Of course he was interested now. Because if what the alpha was saying about holding a child vampire prisoner was true...

"God, I fucking hate werewolves," Xander told him, tone still conversational. "Have I mentioned that yet?"

"Oh, well. Off you flap, then," the leader said, making a shooing motion with one hand. "Nothing stopping you, is there? Not unless you want us to take you to see Junior first..."

Xander gritted his teeth, wanting nothing more at that moment than the human ability to crawl into a bottle, get blind, falling-down drunk, and never crawl back out.

"Fine, Fluffy," he grated. "You win. Take me to see this alleged vampire, and I won't brandish the rolled-up newspaper."

Fluffy's flat, hard eyes were starting to make Xander's skin crawl, quite honestly. But he held back any further insults as Fluffy shrugged a brawny shoulder.

"That's real magnanimous of you, mate," said the werewolf. "Best follow us, in that case. Dawn's coming soon. You wouldn't want to get a terminal case of sunburn, now would you?"

Actually, mate, Xander thought sourly, *you might be surprised. Lately, that prospect has been growing more appealing by the day.*

-o-o-o-

Manisha Sadhu was living a nightmare. With the green-eyed vampire and her other pack members in tow, she followed meekly behind Crank, the alpha werewolf. She and Sangye—the young boy she'd been meant to protect—had been handed to Crank like chattel a couple of weeks ago. Since then, he'd pretty much owned them both, body and soul. Before all this started, Manisha used to think she understood what reality was. She'd known evil existed in the world, of course—these days, you'd have to be blind, deaf, *and* stupid not to realize that evil existed in the world.

But... werewolves? Vampires?

Two weeks ago, she'd been a glorified nanny. No, even that was too generous. She was barely more than a housekeeper, included as part of the small retinue of people helping to hide Sangye in London. She'd been chosen for the position mostly because of her stint in British schools as a teenager and her distant family connections in the UK. After a roadside bomb in Tezpur killed Sangye's Regent and his teachers, he and his remaining retinue fled India for the West in hopes of finding less chaos there.

They should have known better. At first, it seemed that things might work out for them. They had a strong case to offer the Office of Tibet in London when they appealed for asylum, and they'd been awaiting official word while staying in a private house where they would not draw unwanted attention. Then came the terrible evening that would live in Manisha's dreams forever.

4

The sound of fists pounding on the door. A harsh shout to open up for the police. Bhuti, the most senior of Sangye's surviving teachers, had opened the door, saying that there must have been some mistake. Half a dozen black-clad men immediately swarmed in, breaking Bhuti's neck as Manisha watched in horror from the second story balcony.

She still remembered the smell that rose around the intruders like a cloud — in fact, some days she thought she would never be completely free of it. It was the smell of the grave. The smell of death. They moved quickly through the house, choked-off screams marking the senseless murders of the others who had been staying on the first floor.

Manisha ran into Sangye's bedroom and started yanking frantically at the window, trying without success to open it while his mother clasped the boy in her arms and attempted to keep him quiet. She'd hoped that if his mother Jampa held Manisha's legs while she lowered Sangye out by his hands, maybe the two of them could get the six-year-old down safely from the second story. But then it was too late.

One of the men kicked the flimsy bedroom door off its hinges even as Manisha searched around for something heavy enough to break the window's glass. Huge forms rushed in and overpowered them. She struggled, certain that she was about to be killed like the others. A cold laugh came from the open doorway.

"Oh, how utterly delectable," said a voice with an oily Eastern European accent. "You have truly outdone yourself, my Master."

The speaker was tall and broad-shouldered, dressed in sunglasses and a dark, tailored suit that contrasted sharply with the black military gear the other men were wearing. He also didn't appear to be conversing with anyone presently inside the room. A chill skittered its way up Manisha's spine.

Jampa was weeping now, straining toward her son. "Please," she begged in broken English. "Please, no! He is boy… just small boy!"

"Who are you?" Manisha snapped, trying not to gag at the stench now choking the bedroom. "I demand to know what agency or organization you represent!"

The man in the suit came closer, his sunglasses reflecting her frightened face in stereo.

"You *demand*?" he asked, clearly amused. "Well, if you *demand* it of me, then I will tell you that as far as you're concerned, I am here on behalf of the Ministry of Death."

A moan of fear escaped Jampa's throat, and she sagged in her captor's grip. From across the room, Sangye watched the man, wide-eyed, but still maintaining that otherworldly aura of calm and serenity that drew in everyone who met him.

"Why?" the boy asked simply.

The leader regarded him for a long moment, tilting his head as if to get a better look at him. "Because taking a bishop and a queen with a single move is far too tempting an opportunity to ignore." His attention shifted to the goon holding Manisha.

"Cuff that one and take her outside to the van. If she doesn't keep quiet, gag her."

Her captor zip-tied Manisha's hands behind her back and dragged her down the stairs, past Bhuti's broken body, and outside to a waiting black van. Manisha clamped her lips together, not wanting to give the goon an excuse to gag her before they left the house. As soon as they were outside, though, she started shrieking like a banshee for help. Within a second, a meaty, stinking hand slapped across her mouth. She bit down hard on his clammy flesh, choking on the bile that tried to rise, but the man didn't even flinch.

He shoved her into the back of the van and stuffed a wad of cloth in her mouth, tying it in place to keep it there. Manisha's eyes watered, and she jammed herself into the corner, as far away from him as she could get. They stayed like that for what seemed like an age, even though it was probably no more than an hour—if that. Manisha's heart pounded, her head joining in with a throbbing rhythm as time dragged on.

Eventually, the van door opened again, and two more goons squeezed in with Sangye shackled between them. Manisha whimpered around the gag—heavy iron manacles bound the boy's wrists, ankles, and neck. He was fighting them with far more strength than a terrified child should possess; moving and flailing so much that Manisha couldn't get a proper look at him.

Jampa was conspicuously absent.

The goons clipped the heavy chains fastened to the shackles to solid steel rings welded to the van's frame. Manisha's guard situated himself on the bench opposite her in the other front corner of the cargo area. He drew a wicked-looking dagger of some dark metal. It looked like iron, as well, but… who made daggers out of iron? The other two guards released their grip on the chains and stepped quickly down from the back of the van, slamming the doors behind them.

Sangye stilled for an instant, and Manisha drew in a sharp breath when she saw his glowing red eyes in the near-darkness. As if the small noise had drawn his attention, he stared at her for the space of two heartbeats, and lunged. She shrieked in terrified surprise, the noise muffled by the gag. The heavy shackles pulled the boy to a stop less than an arm's length away from her as she scrabbled as far back into the corner as she could get.

The van was moving now. The intermittent sodium-yellow glow of streetlights streaming through the van's tiny, barred windows transformed Sangye's face into something monstrous. There was no recognition in his expression, and his teeth gnashed at the air as he strained toward her. She could see the wicked points of fangs glinting beneath his curled lips as his jaws chomped mindlessly on nothing.

The breath shook loose from her chest in a rush. Manisha started screaming again, the gag absorbing the sound with its smothering bulk. She screamed and screamed, and didn't stop screaming until the goons came back to drag Sangye away from her, still fighting to free himself from the shackles.

Whoever would have guessed that nightmar-ish van ride would only be the beginning? Suit-and-sunglasses had a guard haul her out after Sangye, and the black-clad men deposited them both in an abandoned basement. The place had been fitted with cells that would have been right at home in a dungeon somewhere, but the rest of the building looked like an old warehouse. She hadn't recognized any other buildings or landmarks dur-ing the brief trip from the van to the large double doors leading inside.

She was thrown into an empty cell, and from the horrible growling, choking noises nearby, Sangye had been dragged into the one next to her—probably still shackled, based on the casual way the guards exited and closed the door behind them. Manisha's knees went weak, and she sank down onto the filthy floor, tears squeezing from between her eyelids. She felt horribly lightheaded, and desperately thirsty as the cloth stuffed between her lips leached the moisture from her mouth.

Some time later, the door to her cell opened. She staggered clumsily to her feet, her balance thrown off by her bound hands. In the absence of any other viable plans, she charged toward the path to freedom. A ragged man with an unkempt gray beard grabbed her and held her with effortless strength as she kicked and struggled. Over his shoulder, she caught a glimpse of the Suit, his pasty face twisted in cold amusement behind the concealing dark glasses.

Graybeard dragged her back to the center of the cell, whirled her around in his grip, and buried his teeth in her shoulder, ripping out a chunk of her trapezius muscle. She screamed again, hoarse and muffled by choking cloth. Just as abruptly as he'd attacked, he let her fall to the ground. Pain exploded behind her eyes.

Manisha's consciousness wavered in and out, Graybeard's voice sounding like it was echoing through a tunnel as he growled, "Awright, now give me the damned money. Can't believe you talked me into turning a new bitch for Crank — that mangy bastard."

Her hearing faded, returning a moment later. "...sure this will make it a worthwhile venture for you. Now, leave." That was the Suit's voice, she thought dazedly.

A few more grumbled words, and then one set of footsteps came closer while another departed. A hand — soaked in so much aftershave she could hardly breathe without choking on it — pulled the gag from her mouth.

"*Why?*" she rasped, echoing Sangye's plaintive question from earlier. She could feel blood trickling down her shoulder to pool beneath her.

"Very simple," said the Suit. "You're one of the vampires' whores. I could sense it as soon as I got close to the boy. But your pet nightcrawler will hardly be able to reclaim you under the circumstances. Not now that you're a werewolf." He laughed. "It's so much more of a blow this way. Much better than simply killing you, only for you to be reborn yet again and return as a threat in a few short decades."

A *werewolf*? At the time, she'd tried to dismiss the nonsensical, unbelievable words. Now, some thirteen days later, she knew better. Something inside her had changed the moment she'd been bitten. She felt trapped here with the pack as surely as Sangye was trapped in his iron shackles, and her time was running out. The full moon was in two nights, and according to the others, once she'd transformed into a wolf for the first time, she would never be able to escape this curse.

Even now, the wolf trapped inside her drove her inexorably to stay with the pack. She could feel it cower and bare its throat whenever Crank so much as looked at her. If she had been alone, she knew she would have given into despair and stopped fighting. But it wasn't just herself that she needed to worry about.

Sangye was here, too.

TWO

The day after their capture, Manisha heard Sangye weeping quietly in his cell. Crank came in not long after, supremely confident in his power over her as the alpha wolf. He'd cut the zip-tie binding her hands behind her back; given her food and water. Specifically, he'd given her a joint of some kind of raw meat still clinging to the bone. She'd fallen on it and torn it free in great chunks with her teeth.

Manisha was a vegetarian. She had been one her entire life.

But now, to her horror, she found that she was merely a wolf in human's clothing. After she'd eaten, Crank took her into Sangye's cell and told her to look after him. Told her that he was a vampire now, and would need to drink human blood. He carelessly informed her that he would have a homeless person or a runaway brought in, and instructed her to try and keep Sangye from killing them too fast when he fed.

Then he left, slamming the cell door behind him.

Sangye's face was smeared with rusty tear tracks that looked like old blood. "Kumari Sadhu?" he asked in a rasping voice, addressing her with the same respectful honorific he'd always used. "I have done something unforgivable."

It was so like his old demeanor that she didn't even think. She just stumbled forward and dropped to her knees, wrapping him up in her arms.

"No," she said, her voice sounding watery. "It's the men who took us who have done unforgivable things."

"You're hurt," Sangye murmured. "And you don't smell... right. What happened?"

The throbbing agony in her shoulder had faded to a dull ache with unnatural speed over the course of the hours she'd spent huddled in her cell. The wound should have been debilitating, left untreated as it had been. Yet she'd almost forgotten about it upon seeing Sangye.

"I'm all right," she managed. "Don't worry about it. Something has been... done to us, and I don't understand it. But I swear to you that I'll protect you and get us out of here somehow."

Even then, the fear she'd felt at the prospect of leaving this place—of disobeying the alpha werewolf who'd brought her food and told her to care for Sangye—made her realize that her words could well be a lie.

She told herself that going along with the leader was just smart strategy. She would ingratiate herself. Gain his trust. It only made sense, right? Inside, though, she worried that if and when an opportunity came, whatever shred of humanity she had left wouldn't be strong enough for her to take action. But she *had* to be strong enough. She had to be strong for Sangye. She'd just given him her word, after all.

As promised, Crank delivered a shaking teen-age boy to the cell less than a day after he'd said he would. Sangye only closed his eyes and turned his head away, though Manisha could see the glint of fangs peeking out from under his upper lip in the harsh light of the naked bulb overhead. She had tried to share some of her meager ration of food and water with him, but he could barely choke it down. Anything he did manage to swallow came right back up.

At first, Crank was impatient. He slashed the kidnapped teen's arm with a switchblade and pressed the sluggishly bleeding cut against Sang-ye's mouth as his victim wailed and begged. Again and again, Sangye only turned away and clamped his lips together tightly. On the fourth day, he met the teenager's eyes with his glowing ones after re-fusing the blood. A moment later, the struggling adolescent went calm and still, the fear draining from him like water from cupped hands.

Crank gave Sangye a narrow-eyed stare and shrugged. "Suit yourself, pipsqueak," he said. "You'll give in before you starve to death, I'll wa-ger."

Knowing Sangye as she did, Manisha wasn't so sure about that, but she kept her doubts to her-self.

"Why are we keeping him here like this, any-way?" she asked, caught as always between the part of her that insisted the word 'we' was a part of her ruse to gain Crank's trust, and the part that thought it sounded quite natural to lump herself in with the other werewolves. "What do you need him for?"

"Bait," Crank said. "For a bigger fish." He smiled down at her and lifted a large, callused hand, brushing a strand of Manisha's hair back and hooking it over her ear.

And that was when she realized she had even more problems than she'd previously realized.

Though she felt hopelessly alone in her unfolding predicament, the reality was that the warehouse teemed with werewolves. The others in the pack came and talked with her sometimes. Really, she thought they came to gawp at Sangye, but at least they talked to her while they did it.

That was how she'd learned that unless the man who'd bitten her died before the next full moon, she'd be stuck as a werewolf forever once she'd undergone her first transformation. It was also how she learned that Crank used to have a lover—his mate, the others called her—but that she'd been killed a few months ago. The middle-aged woman who'd shared that particular bit of gossip had looked at Manisha with an air of speculation as she spoke.

And now Manisha knew why.

Crank started making little possessive gestures like that whenever he was around her over the next few days. Each time he did, the wolf in her preened, even as the human in her quailed. After the full moon, would she mindlessly fall into the arms of this creature who thought nothing of kidnapping innocents and keeping a six-year-old child manacled in a cell? Would the last trace of her free will be lost with the turning of the lunar month?

Desperation clawed at her, yet she was no closer to having a useful plan of escape than she'd been on the night Graybeard had torn a bloody chunk from her shoulder and changed her. She could try to run, fighting her new pack instincts all the way, but she didn't know where the key to Sangye's shackles was being kept. She had no way to free him from this place, and she feared that even if the police believed her far-fetched story, by the time she got anyone in the outside world to take action, Crank would simply have pulled up stakes and moved somewhere else.

And all that didn't even take Mr. Suit-and-Sunglasses into account. He'd known exactly where Sangye was being kept, even though the location of the private house where they were staying was supposedly secret. Add in the goons' military garb, and who knew whether the police and government could be trusted to help her in the first place?

The next morning, Crank called the pack together to talk to them.

"All right, you lot," he said, his voice booming around the empty warehouse. "We've got us another vamp to catch. My contact says one of the bloodsuckers is definitely in London. We need to find him and draw him here."

"Does your bloke know where he is?" asked one of the men—a grizzle-haired old grump who called himself Patch.

"Just that he's in this area," Crank said. "If Kovac gets close enough to pin down this nightcrawler's exact location, then the nightcrawler will be able to sense Kovac in turn, and he'll know he's being watched. It's up to us to stake out the likely spots where a freak might go to feel right at home. You all know the drill. We'll start looking tonight. And when we find him—" Crank's eyes fell on Manisha, pinning her, "—I want Brown Eyes here to draw him out into the open."

Manisha's heart beat faster. It was a test of her loyalty to the pack, she knew, and she probably didn't want to know what would happen if she failed it. But could it also be an opportunity in disguise? How crazy would she have to be to run away from werewolves, and straight into the arms of a vampire?

Yet... she'd held a vampire in her arms these last many nights. She'd held a small boy. He'd been turned into the ravenous monster she'd seen in the van, true. Now, though, he was to all appearances the same sweet child he'd been before. A serene, loving boy who refused to drink the blood of innocents even as he slowly starved to death.

"Why does this contact of yours want to catch vampires, anyway?" she asked.

Crank gave her a sour look. "No idea, luv. All I care about is that there's money and power at stake. Working with him is good for the pack, and if it's good for the pack, then it's what we do."

And so, several days later, that was how Manisha found herself marching back from a nightclub in Lambeth toward the warehouse in Battersea along with a dozen werewolves and one very brassed-off vampire. A note bearing a hastily scribbled plea for help burned a hole in her pocket. She'd spent the last hour second-guessing herself over the contents and handling of that note. She probably should have slipped the wad of paper to the vampire when she first approached him in the club, but she'd told herself she wanted to get a look at him first, and see if she could feel him out a bit before deciding whether or not to trust him.

Then she'd told herself that giving the note to him while they were still in the club would mess up Crank's plan and expose her, because she hadn't thought to write "play along" at the end of the short message. He'd have paused to read it, probably questioned her, and Manisha wasn't stupid enough to think that Crank didn't have someone in the club watching her every move.

On the walk to Battersea, she felt too exposed. The others were all around them. They'd see if she tried to pass something to him. And to make it worse, she still had no idea if she could even trust him or not. In the club, he'd been cold and brusque when he thought she was seeking help for her injured sister. When Crank and the others arrived, he'd been openly hostile.

But he'd also been completely un-cowed by Crank's presence. Indeed, he was the first person she'd seen who didn't show the alpha werewolf the slightest bit of deference. Or the slightest bit of respect, for that matter. Watching the vampire's careless disregard for the pack of werewolves hemming him in, Manisha had felt her pulse speed up, though she couldn't have said if it was with dread or excitement. Would this pale, handsome creature truly be powerful enough to back up his casual arrogance, if it came down to it?

Could he get Sangye away to safety somehow? Protect him from Crank and the others? She decided with sudden certainty that he was the best chance she was likely to get. She would have to beat back the cowering wolf inside her long enough for her human self to take this gamble.

Her chance came as they were descending the dark staircase leading to the warehouse basement. She positioned herself near the vampire, suddenly wishing that she had some sort of a background in either sleight of hand or pick-pocketing. He was understandably wary of his surroundings, his eyes glowing with an unnatural green light in the dim illumination.

Crank was ahead of them, not looking back, and the others were giving the vampire a healthy bubble of space inside the enclosed area. With a deep breath, Manisha eased the sloppily folded paper scrap out of her battered jeans, and tried to judge the best moment to slip it into his pocket.

He stiffened as her hand brushed the fabric of his tailored trousers, and her breath stuttered. God, how had she ever thought she could be subtle enough to pull off something like this? His hand darted out with inhuman speed, clasping her wrist in an uncompromising grip. Without warning, electricity jolted through her like she'd been struck by lightning. She gasped and jerked free, nearly tripping down the stairs in her haste.

She cast around with wide eyes. Panic gripped her throat as she became abruptly aware that every gaze in the stairwell was now pinned on her… and on the vampire who was standing two steps above her, staring down at her with shocked green eyes.

THREE

Xander's first thought when the jolt of raw pow-er went through him was *no*. His second thought was also *no*. And his third thought was *oh, fuck no*.

All eyes were on the pair of them as they stood staring at each other in consternation. The woman recovered first. She surged up the steps separating them and slapped him full across the face with a strength that seemed less than werewolf, somehow, though it was certainly more than a human of her size should have been able to muster.

It was a toss-up what was more distracting—the shock of electricity as their skin connected, or the flare of pain as her nails dug furrows in his cheek. His hiss of surprise was unfeigned, but her strategy wasn't a bad one under the circumstances. Circumstances, he realized, which could hardly be worse. He'd felt her slip something into his trouser pocket, and now he could just about detect the crinkle of paper inside. A note?

There was no way to confirm it right now—Fluffy was already charging up the steps two at a time, his face locked in a scowl. The other were-wolves looked on uncertainly.

"He tried to grab me!" his erstwhile damsel in distress accused, her mahogany eyes flashing fire.

With difficulty, Xander rallied his wits enough to play along with the game, even if he didn't know yet what the stakes were. Or what the rules were, come to that.

"She got too close," he said, in an approximation of the same cold, bored tone he'd used in the alley. "Keep your puppies under control, mate. This shirt is fucking *Versace*. I don't need someone shedding on it."

The werewolf alpha moved the woman aside — not gently, but also not with undue force — and then he was in Xander's face. Despite Xander being a step higher on the stairs, they were more or less eye-to-eye. Somewhat to his surprise, he felt testosterone-fueled anger rising in his chest at the open challenge from another male, even if it was a male from the wrong fucking species. The primitive reaction threatened to belie Xander's *cold, superior bastard* act, even though it would be the height of foolishness to engage with this prick in a stairwell while surrounded by ten other hostile-looking werewolves.

Still, the choice to dissipate into mist when a meaty hand closed on the front of the aforementioned Versace shirt was a shockingly difficult one to make in the face of his desire to start removing body parts instead. Or, at least, in the face of his desire to *attempt* removing body parts. Xander had never actually brawled with a two-meter-tall alpha werewolf before, and had no idea how the brute's strength would match up against a hundred-year-old vampire's.

This, he told himself very firmly, was obviously not the time or the place to find out, no matter what his instincts were screaming. He materialized at the base of the stairs, striving for *cool and unruffled* rather than *flustered, pissed off, and in desperate need of a drink*. Interestingly, he realized that the marks of the woman's nails on his left cheek had not immediately started to heal.

"Holding your little prisoner back here somewhere, are you?" he asked, as the flicker of a weak, vampiric presence teased his awareness. With an effort of will, he put aside the inconceivable revelation he'd just experienced a moment ago in favor of the thing he'd originally come here to investigate. Even so, he felt hyper-aware of the crinkling paper square nestled in his pocket... and of the female werewolf now emerging from the stairwell.

Xander didn't wait for Fluffy to answer, or for the others to catch up with him. The shadowy presence inside his mind was its own guide. He reached out mentally, moving toward it.

Can you hear me? he sent, and received a faint sense of confusion or query in reply.

The weakened vampire was in a cell near the far end of the underground level. Xander dissipated again, flowing through the small, barred window set in the heavy door. He reformed to find a boy of perhaps six or seven manacled to the concrete wall with iron. The child looked awful — emaciated and frightened. His dark eyes were defined by the graceful sweep of epicanthic folds, and his face would have been soft and round if not for the hollows under his cheeks.

Xander's immediate thought was, *his essence feels like Snag's...* but that was ridiculous. The child before him was freshly turned and desperately fragile—about as far from the millennia-old, silent head-case of a vampire he'd left back in Damascus in terms of age and power as it was possible to be.

"You're like me," the boy rasped in accented English.

"So it would seem," he said, a bit faintly. Outside the cell, he could hear cursing and the scraping of keys. "Quickly, now—I can feel that you need blood."

He crossed the distance separating them and offered his wrist. The boy's face twisted up.

"No," he whispered, to Xander's consternation.

"Why—" Xander began, only to be cut off when the door clanged open. Fluffy stood in the gap, an iron dagger held in one meaty paw. Behind him stood six other burly male werewolves, similarly armed.

"Get him," the alpha snarled, and lunged through the door.

Xander growled in frustration. "Oh, for god's sake—"

In the absence of intelligent alternatives, he dissipated for a third time and rushed toward the aboveground level of the warehouse before Fluffy could decide to do something predictable—like threatening the boy if Xander didn't return to human form.

I'll come back, I promise, he sent as he swirled away, adding, *hang in there, kid,* only to wince at the *faux pas* an instant later as he remembered the iron shackles.

There were several broken windows on the ground floor that no one had bothered to board up yet. Beyond them, the sun was poised to rise above London's jagged skyline. Since the alternative to making a run for it was to hover around the ceiling of the warehouse all day hiding from the mongrels, Xander flew a couple of blocks over, riding the wind currents and keeping to the shadows. Thankfully, he slipped through a ventilation pipe in a convenient office building before the first rays of sun could singe him.

Inside, he found a comfortable looking corner office, did a quick scout for security cameras, and reformed into solidity when he didn't find any. A couple of quick flicks drew the blinds across the large windows, cutting off the threat of the encroaching morning light. According to the clock on the wall, it was barely after five a.m. Figuring he was unlikely to be disturbed as long as he kept half an ear out for the maintenance staff, he flopped down in the desk chair.

Under the circumstances, leaving had clearly been the only reasonable thing to do. A long-buried streak of stubborn male ego had tried to goad him into attacking Fluffy in the stairwell. Now, the same stubborn streak insisted that leaving the woman and the boy behind felt an awful lot like running away with his tail between his legs.

In his defense, Xander had always enjoyed a good brawl—even more so, now that it would take a stake through the heart or decapitation to put him down and out for good. *At least, you enjoy it when the creatures you're brawling with aren't wearing the bodies of children while they shoot and hack at you,* noted the treacherous voice in the back of his mind, memories of his recent stint in Haiti floating to the surface.

That insidious little voice was one he'd spent decades quieting with whatever exotic chemicals he could find conveniently swimming in a nearby human's bloodstream. Unfortunately, the *better living through chemistry* option was off the table at the moment. His mouth twisted in displeasure. Pushing everything else to the side in favor of trying to figure out the current situation, he let out a sigh and kicked back to rest his feet on the edge of the desk. The note was still in his pocket. He pulled it out and unfolded it, examining it.

The paper was an irregular shape — dusty, torn on two edges, previously crumpled, and smelling faintly of werewolf. One side was covered with faded writing in pencil. It appeared to be someone's quick and dirty mathematical calculations, partially missing where the scrap had been torn from the larger page. He turned it over. The writing on the other side was much clearer, though it had been written with a cheap pen that was running out of ink.

THE CHILD AND I ARE BOTH PRISONERS
PLEASE HELP US GET AWAY — MEET ME IN
THE SAME ALLEY AS BEFORE AT MIDNIGHT
TONIGHT

He tossed the paper onto the desk, once more drawn back to the elephant in the room. The one part of this fiasco that he really, *really* wasn't ready to acknowledge. The woman. She had been his—

No. He couldn't do anything about that right now. Practicality—that was the key.

So... stick to the practical parts. The proposed meeting didn't seem terribly likely to be a trap. And even if it was, no matter how many mongrels decided to show up to the party, he could always slip from their grasp the same way he'd done this morning—by flying away. If they had any fancier tricks to use on him, they'd have used them when they had him on their turf, surely. They didn't even appear to have firearms. If they had, they could have riddled him with bullets when they had the chance, in an attempt to weaken him too much for him to be able to transform into mist.

Given those facts, he'd lay odds that the note was genuine. His fingers grazed the four parallel scratches on his cheek—still open and raw more than half an hour after she'd struck him.

She'd been smart. Quick-thinking. *Beautiful*, his mind supplied without prompting.

A werewolf, he reminded himself sharply. *She'd been a fucking werewolf.*

And what the hell was he supposed to do about *that* tiny little wrinkle? He realized with a growl of irritation that he was—yet again—thinking about the one thing he didn't want to think about. He pulled out his mobile and powered it on.

There were three more messages from Tré's number waiting for him since their brief text exchange earlier. He chewed his lip for a moment, mulling over his options before he decided on a number and dialed. The call picked up on the fourth ring.

"Eris, mate," he said without preamble, "we've got a problem."

"*Xander?*" Eris sounded as though he'd just woken up. A sleepy, feminine murmur came from somewhere close by the phone's pickup, which in no way made something in Xander's chest go tight and achy. Eris cleared his throat and continued, "*Just a moment. Let me send Trynn to get the others.*"

Eris whispered something quietly to his mate. Xander gritted his teeth and very carefully did not listen closely enough to catch the details of the gentle exchange.

"*Oksana, Mason, and Duchess are in Singapore,*" Eris continued in a louder voice, sounding more awake now. "*You knew that, right? The rest of us are here, though. Tré said you were in London?*"

"Yes," Xander said tightly.

"*You shouldn't have gone off alone.*" There was more worry than censure in Eris' voice, but even so—

"Save it. I don't need another installment of the babysitting lecture right now."

There was a short pause.

"*You said there was a problem?*"

Xander let his feet fall back to the worn carpet and leaned forward, resting an elbow on the desk and pinching his thumb and forefinger around the bridge of his nose. "Yes, but I lied. There are actually two problems."

More silence.

He sighed. "Right. So… there's a little baby vampire trapped here, being held by a pack of werewolves. A young boy. The kid's maybe… seven years old or so? If that? Freshly turned, and weak. He's not feeding."

The voice on the other end of the line cursed sharply in Greek.

"They've got him shackled to a wall with iron, Eris," Xander continued. The phone was moving against his ear, and he realized that his hands were shaking. He gripped the mobile harder and pinched the bridge of his nose until it hurt. "It's obvious he's either too weak or not skilled enough yet to transform into mist and escape." He swallowed, trying to wet his dry throat. "I… *Christ*. I left him there."

Bugger. He hadn't actually meant to say that last part out loud.

The pause on Eris' end was shorter this time. *"Well, what else were you going to do, under the circumstances? Look. Just stay put, will you? Preferably somewhere you can keep the place they're holding him under surveillance — if you can do so safely. We'll come to you and go in en masse to retrieve him."*

"Can't—sorry," Xander said shortly. "Not unless you lot can crawl out of that hellhole you're wallowing in and get here in the next nineteen hours."

"Nineteen hours? Why nineteen hours?" Eris' response sounded wary.

Xander snorted. "I mentioned two problems, right? I sort of… ran into Eliza this morning."

"*Eliza? Your mate? Xander, that's —*"

"She's a werewolf," he interrupted. His stomach churned, as though saying the words aloud made it real somehow.

"*She's — ?*"

"A werewolf. You heard me." Xander paused, scrubbing at his closed eyelids. "And she's connected somehow to the boy. She managed to sneak a message to me this morning without the other mongrels noticing. She claims they're holding her there against her will. I'm supposed to meet her privately at midnight."

There was a small disturbance on Eris' end and a new voice spoke. "*Tovarăş.*"

Xander ground his jaw. "Tré."

He could hear Tré draw breath to speak, only to hold it for a long moment.

"*Nothing any of us say is going to sway you from your intended actions, I assume,*" he said eventually.

"No, it won't."

"*We're still coming. We'll be there as soon as is practical.*"

"Of course." Xander dragged his mind back to logic. "So… somebody had better jot all this down. The boy is being held in the basement of the abandoned warehouse at the corner of Gwynne and Harroway Roads in Battersea. My meeting tonight is in the alley behind the back entrance of *Club Cirque,* under the arches off Lambeth Road. And I intend to return to the flat in Mayfair afterward.

That's where you can meet me unless you hear otherwise."

The sound of an elevator door opening down the hall teased his hearing, followed by the squeak of metal wheels.

"Look," he told Tré, "I need to go. I'm squatting in someone's corner office, and I can hear a janitor's cart coming my way." His lip curled in distaste. "Nothing like the smell of lemony fresh disinfectant to lend a bit of bouquet to breakfast, I suppose. Maybe I can convince the bloke to sniff something interesting from an aerosol can before I drink him."

"*Be careful tonight, Xander,*" Tré said, ignoring his foul-tempered grumbling. "*You'll help no one by doing something reckless.*"

He scoffed. "Reckless? Me? These are *were-wolves*, Tré. I can always fly away if things start to get too frisky." The janitor's cart was getting closer now, accompanied by the sound of cheerful, off-key whistling. "Sounds like breakfast is served. Let me know when the five of you are en route. I'll see you when you get here."

With a tap of his thumb, he disconnected the call. The door opened. Xander looked up to find a stooped, middle-aged man standing there staring at him from the doorway, open-mouthed and frozen with surprise.

"Morning, old chap," Xander said, his eyes glowing green. "I'll wager there aren't many people who can say this to someone who cleans public restrooms for a living, but I believe I've dealt with even more shit so far this morning than you have.

Now, tell me... how would you like to make an easy twenty quid in the next five minutes?"

FOUR

Manisha didn't dare act like anything was out of the ordinary after her bizarre reaction to touching the vampire in the stairwell that morning. The day dragged by as she first pretended to nap with the other werewolves, and then busied herself trying unsuccessfully to convince Sangye to feed. She was worried for him. She was terrified for him, in fact, but she had no idea what to do beyond following through with her reckless plan to meet the vampire tonight.

What could possibly have caused that violent jolt when his skin had brushed hers? And again, when she'd struck him? It wasn't just the fact that he was a vampire, since she felt nothing of the sort when she touched Sangye. It hadn't only been a physical shock, either. The instant their hands connected, Manisha's past lives had flashed before her eyes fast enough to leave her dizzy.

Manisha had been raised in a culture where reincarnation was an accepted fact of life. Ever since she was a child, she'd had a clearer recollection than most people of her past existences. Many of them had been filled with troubles; a few had been short and undeniably tragic. One of them in particular had haunted her dreams on a regular basis when she was growing up. It was always hazy and unclear, yet *that* was the life which had leapt free from the background noise of centuries when the vampire grabbed her wrist.

She'd looked into his striking green eyes and felt the oddest flash of recognition... but then reality intruded. She did the first thing she could think of to throw Crank and the others off the scent. She'd struck him full across the face.

She hadn't meant her nails to score red slashes into his pale, ivory-colored cheek. It was as though the wolf had taken over, curling her fingers into claws that tore flesh. Manisha shivered. Tonight was her last chance at salvation before the full moon tomorrow. Yet, she still didn't even know the name of the wolf who'd turned her, much less where he might be found or how he might be killed.

Even in that, she knew she was probably deluding herself. If she blinked and opened her eyes to find the gray-bearded werewolf standing before her and a gun with silver bullets in her hand, did she seriously think she'd be able to look her attacker in the eye and pull the trigger? Assuming the old chestnut about werewolves and silver bullets was even true.

All of this perfectly highlighted how pathetic she was. She'd been too squeamish and frightened to ask the other werewolves about their species' vulnerabilities. How could she possibly expect to be strong enough to take advantage of those vulnerabilities—if they even existed?

She'd watched a man—a *vampire*—vanish into a puff of mist and reappear seconds later. The rational world had been pulled from beneath her feet like a threadbare rug. The best she could hope for at this point was to find some kind of help for Sangye. If nothing else, he should be with his own kind. They would help him, wouldn't they? Surely other vampires wouldn't hold him in a cell, bound in heavy metal shackles that left blistering red marks on his skin like burns where they touched.

She would wait and sneak away, no matter how much the wolf in her whined and howled at the prospect of acting against the pack. Crank had no plans for them to search the city again tonight. From what she gathered, the pack leader was awaiting word from his so-called *contact* about what he should do next.

So, she bided her time, following the same schedule she'd fallen into over the past two weeks. Sleeping, eating, spending time with Sangye. Chatting about nothing of import with the others in the pack who were willing to talk with her. Avoiding Crank... though she thought she felt his cold gaze on her at several points throughout the day. She didn't look up; avoiding eye contact with him, just as her wolf insisted that she do.

Finally, at about ten o'clock at night, she slipped away. The warehouse door was padlocked, she knew, but it was more for appearances than anything, since the others all knew the combination. Besides, several of the ground floor windows were shattered. Crank didn't need locks to keep his pack members from wandering. They were *his pack*, after all. They weren't going anywhere—not really.

It had taken her quite awhile to understand that concept properly. The others weren't prisoners. Well, they were—of a sort—but their prison was one that existed within, not without. The others came and went as they pleased unless the alpha needed them for something. They submitted to him because he was the leader, and he was the leader because they submitted to him.

At any time, one of the other males could have attacked Crank and challenged his position as alpha of the pack. If the challenger won, he would become the new alpha. If he lost, Manisha suspected he would be dead soon afterward—Crank didn't strike her as the type to be forgiving of such a thing.

The point was, no one was *guarding* her, as such. Crank seemed supremely confident of her wolf's power over her human self, and of his power over her wolf. She was bound to the pack, and to him as alpha. He didn't think she was strong enough to fight those instincts.

Tonight, she was bound and determined to prove him wrong about that.

She waited until no one appeared to be paying her any particular attention. After heading casually toward the disgusting basement lavatory, she doubled back to the stairwell and kept to the shadows. She tiptoed up the stairs, every rustle of clothing and squeak of her shoes sounding amplified to her own ears.

Once on the ground level, she looked around nervously and headed straight for the nearest broken window, using her sleeve wrapped around her hand to remove enough of the jagged hunks of glass that she could shimmy through it without slicing herself to ribbons. Only when she was outside, her shoes crunching on broken glass, did she release the breath she'd been holding.

Wrong, wrong, stop, this is wrong, her instincts howled. She grit her teeth. *No,* she insisted. *What's wrong is chaining a little boy to a wall with shackles that burn his flesh. What's wrong is kidnapping and killing innocent people. Turning them into monsters!*

She realized with dismay that she was still standing by the open window like a statue, arguing silently with herself instead of running away. She turned and fled into the night.

-o-o-o-

Three more times, Manisha caught herself huddling in doorways or dark alleys, mentally debating her course of action. It was insidious, the way her mind was turning against itself, things inside her changing without her conscious awareness. On each occasion, some noise or movement at the corner of her eye would snap her back to her surroundings, and she would push that treacherous inner voice to one side so she could continue.

She'd thought she was leaving plenty of time to walk the six or so kilometers between Battersea and Lambeth, but her bouts of lapsing into a fugue state while she battled her instincts meant that she would have barely thirty minutes to spare by the time she arrived. She'd wanted to stake the place out for an hour or so... wait for the vampire to get there so she could watch him and try to gauge a bit more about him before she made herself known.

Would he come alone? Were there other vampires in London?

Yet again, her feet stumbled to a stop without her permission, while that crafty inner voice sowed fresh doubts about her course of action. She almost snarled aloud in frustration. Fortunately, the railway arch concealing the club entrance was within sight now. Anger propelled her the final few hundred meters—up to the next block, around the corner and into the warren of alleys beyond the rails.

A whiff of musky odor hit her nose, and large hands closed on her arms from both sides. She choked on a shriek, heart pounding, surprise stealing her breath. She hadn't heard a thing as they'd approached. Her eyes darted from one side to the other. Two of the males from Crank's pack held her securely between them. One was Tag—she'd spoken to him a few times, and he'd seemed a pleasant sort. She hadn't had much interaction with the red-haired man on her right, but she'd heard people call him Sawbones, and gathered he was one of Crank's most trusted lieutenants.

"Let me go!" she demanded, jerking her arms in their grip to no avail. Had they followed her all the way here without her even noticing? They must have done, and the thought sickened her.

"You shouldn't have run, Manisha," Tag said. She thought she detected a hint of regret beneath the words, but his manner was no-nonsense.

"I'm not Crank's property!" she nearly shouted. Her voice echoed around the dark alley, but there was no one nearby to hear it.

"Close enough to it," Sawbones growled.

Tag's voice was a bit calmer, but his grip on her arm never wavered. "It's complicated, pet. Things'll make more sense in a couple of days, once you've changed for the first time."

Sawbones gave her arm a little shake. "Who are you meeting here, girl? The vampire? Crank thought you might, after that scene at the warehouse," he said, his tone unyielding as his eyes bored into hers.

Manisha couldn't stop her gaze from sliding down and away, but she clamped her lips to keep the treacherous wolf from spilling everything to the sharp-eyed man staring down at her.

"Eh, why am I even bothering? Of course it's the vampire," Sawbones muttered, and shifted his attention to Tag. "She was obviously heading for the same dead-end alley from last night. Wait there for the bloodsucker, and give him the message like Crank said."

Tag looked nervous, but he just nodded and said, "Yeah, okay." The glance he threw Manisha as he let her arm go was a bit worried. A bit sad.

"You," Sawbones said, jerking her other arm roughly. "You're coming with me."

Her wolf wanted nothing more than to roll over in defeat, baring its neck. It was all she could do to plant her feet and glare at him. "What's to stop me from yelling *fire* or *rape* at the top of my lungs, you bastard?"

Sawbones snorted and gestured at the dark warren with his free hand. "Go right ahead. 'Round here, you'll probably just attract a crowd to watch."

She sucked in a breath, ready to take her chances, but he continued. "Oh, stop it. Save your damned breath, an' my ears while you're at it. Unless you want bad things to happen to your little vampy boy back at the warehouse, you'll keep your trap shut and come along quietly."

Manisha's heart stuttered.

"Crank gave you a chance, luv," Sawbones continued, "and you threw it in his face. He won't be too pleased. Best come back and take your lashes. Chances are he won't come down too hard on your pretty little arse since he's wanting you for a mate once you change over. But he doesn't like vamps, so I doubt he'll go so easy on the sprog if you raise a fuss and make trouble."

The fact that Crank had obviously been onto her since the scene in the stairwell felt like a lead weight in Manisha's stomach. She sagged, defeated. There was no point in trying to stall her captor—the vampire wasn't due to arrive for another half hour or more. There was no one here to help her. If she let Sawbones take her back to Crank, there would at least be a chance she could talk the alpha into punishing her personally rather than taking out his frustrations on Sangye.

Maybe if she played nice with him, she could eventually gain Crank's trust again. Find out what he was planning for Sangye with his mysterious contact in the black suit and sunglasses. Bide her time… wait for a better chance.

Yes, her wolf agreed. *That's right. Better to just go along with the pack.*

She cast a last, hopeless glance around the dingy surroundings, but there was no one here except her and her two captors.

"All right," she whispered, hating herself. "I'll come."

FIVE

The great barred owl was not the most inconspicuous sight in the sky over Lambeth at night, perhaps, but it was silent and sharp-eyed. Those two qualities were what Xander needed right now. The owl brought a different sort of awareness of one's surroundings than did a cloud of formless mist. And right now, he felt like a hunter.

He'd wanted to scope out the area around the meeting place before the woman — whom he refused to think of as Eliza — arrived. Courtesy of Murphy's Law, that plan culminated in Eris ringing him right as he'd been about to leave. The other vampire had passed on details of their travel itinerary, which was admittedly important information — but it had still detained Xander longer than he'd intended.

The others had managed to arrange a patchwork of private and public transport that would get them out of the beleaguered Middle East and into the UK before dawn on the day after tomorrow.

Hooray for them.

The practical upshot was that Xander reached the skies above *Club Cirque* with around twenty minutes to spare. Less than he would have liked, but thankfully still enough to get an owl's eye view of whatever awaited him before he committed to going through with the meeting. The gray buildings that formed the alleyways behind the back entrance of the club were mostly three stories tall or less, so it was easy enough to get a good look at the narrow passageways between them as he soared overhead. He rode the rising currents of warm air from the city below, his wings barely beating.

He traced the area, working his way from the outside in, scouting the maze with an eye toward identifying any obvious traps. The alleys were mostly devoid of any life larger than the occasional stray dog or cat. Rats darted here and there, scavenging through garbage. He noted two homeless people camped some distance from each other. Neither of them was particularly close to the cul-de-sac behind the *Cirque*. One of them was so old and emaciated that Xander discounted him as a threat. The other was a teenage girl, and while he could not discount her being a werewolf, she was poorly placed to attack, and unquestionably alone.

At last, with five minutes or so remaining before midnight, he flew over the meeting place itself. A single figure lounged against the wall near the alley mouth, arms folded as he scanned his surroundings. Almost certainly a werewolf; most definitely not Eliz—

Most definitely not the woman.

He tucked his wings and dove into the shadowed dead end, giving a couple of strong flaps to slow his descent and transforming to drop lightly onto his feet, standing across from the scruffy man.

The werewolf pushed away from the wall, his stance wary, but he did not immediately attack. Xander inhaled, scenting the air — one thing the owl was fairly useless at doing. Other wolves had been here. Not in this alley, but nearby. Their scents were already fading away, dissipating into the larger tapestry of London's back-alley stench. Still, he thought one of the mingled odors was the same one that had exploded in his nostrils when the woman struck him, leaving behind the four red lines that still decorated his face, unhealed nearly a full day later.

"Hello. You know, if you're supposed to be the trap, mate, your pack might want to consider bringing in a strategy consultant," Xander said, eyeing the slender, dark-haired man.

"Not a trap," said the werewolf. "Just a messenger. You're here for Manisha, right?"

"Manisha? Is that her name?" Xander asked. Something thin and wickedly sharp pricked at his heart, the point coated in a poisonous slurry of dread and old pain.

"She won't be coming," said the werewolf. "Crank says if you want to see her or the vampire kid alive, come to 314 Tedwin Mews in Stockwell at dusk tonight."

Xander grabbed the werewolf by his shirtfront and slammed him roughly against the alley wall before he could so much as blink. "Who the fuck is Crank?"

The lad — for that was what he was, not yet twenty and not long turned — paled under Xander's glowing green glare. To his credit, though, his voice didn't quake when he answered.

"You met him," he said. "The pack alpha."

"You mean Fluffy?" Xander grated. "I should've brought out the damned newspaper when I had the chance." His hand tightened, lifting the smaller man until his toes barely touched the ground. "Tell me, who did you piss off to get thrown under the bus like this?"

"When someone higher up in the pack tells you to do something, you do it."

Xander wished the little punk would fight back, and give him an excuse for violence. But he just hung there in Xander's grip, looking vaguely uncomfortable as the menacing silence stretched between them.

"Look," the werewolf said eventually, "I shouldn't tell you this. But if I were you, I'd just walk away. I don't claim to know why Crank's dragging us into this vampire shit, but I know it's bad news. So… just leave London, okay? Forget about the baby vamp. Forget about Manisha. Crank wants her for a mate once she's undergone her first full moon. That much I do know. I don't think he's really gonna kill her."

Unthinking rage the likes of which he couldn't remember feeling in decades flooded Xander's vision, turning it red. "*He wants her for what?*" he hissed, every word filled with deadly intent.

The werewolf obviously heard the threat of murder lurking behind the question, and his already pale face went chalky and bloodless. "I… I just meant—"

Xander realized with a jolt that he was about a second away from breaking the boy's neck. Which… might or might not be possible, since he was a werewolf, and which almost certainly wouldn't kill him. And, like a dimwit, Xander had neglected to return to his Mayfair flat after leaving the office building in Battersea at sunset. His flat… where the weapons collection in the spare bedroom contained, among other things, a case full of artistically wrought silver blades.

Xander could *probably* pummel the punk in his grip into the dirt, given that he was young, small, and in human form. But doing so would only be for the sake of dishing out pain. It wouldn't do a damned thing to change the situation. And, besides, the little sod had just given him free advice that would have been quite reasonable in other circumstances.

He forced the killing rage back into something a little more manageable. A moment later, the distant, nauseating wash of self-disgust that he usually quieted with chemical assistance reared its unwelcome head to fill the gap. Too bad chemical assistance wasn't going to be an option anytime soon.

He took a slow breath.

"Dusk, you said? To hell with that," he said. "You and I are taking a trip to Stockwell right the fuck now."

The werewolf gasped as Xander spun him around and pinned him face first against the wall with one arm twisted painfully up his back. "It won't make a difference," the kid mumbled into the filthy brickwork.

"Shut it," Xander replied, pulling his phone from his pocket to call up a map one-handed.

Stockwell had been a well-to-do hamlet at the edge of London when he'd still been human, but these days it was an uncomfortable mix of elegant old Victorian houses and grotty council estates. He'd not had much cause to spend time there, honestly. Making a quick decision, he used his larger frame to hold the werewolf in place while he hailed a ride on the Lyft app.

"Bloody Christ, I still miss Uber sometimes," he muttered. Then, louder, "Come on. Shift your mangy arse."

He manhandled the teenager toward the alley leading onto Carlisle Lane, keeping him in an unforgiving hammerlock with his arm twisted behind him. It was hit or miss whether dragging someone through the streets of South London like this in the middle of the night would cause any sort of problem, the way things were in the city these days. With the addition of a bit of vampiric suggestion, however, it became a complete non-issue.

Only two people bothered to give them a second look as Xander made his way to their pickup point at Carlisle and Royal Street. After a mental nudge convinced them that they had not, in fact, seen anything alarming, neither one gave Xander and his hostage a third look.

Similarly, when the white Nissan Leaf pulled up next to the curb, the look of startlement and dawning fear on the driver's face smoothed into serenity a moment later.

Xander might have been the youngest of the original vampires by about a century, but he'd always had a talent for mind control. Which... well. Everyone needed a hobby, right?

"Don't bother getting the door, luv. I've got it," he said grimly, and shoved his prisoner into the back seat—making a cursory attempt at not banging his head against the frame. There was no reason to dent such a shiny and eco-friendly car, after all.

Once they were all settled, the woman glanced back in the rearview mirror. "314 Tedwin Mews, right?" she asked. "In Stockwell?"

"Yes," Xander said. "Quick as you can, please."

The car rejoined the sporadic traffic, its electric engine eerily quiet. The driver filled the silence with idle chitchat about the latest bomb scares and riots, her chirpy tone at odds with both the circumstances and the subject matter.

The werewolf shot Xander a side-eyed glance. "So... you do realize that the hypnotism thing is creepy as hell, right?" he asked.

"Fuck off," Xander said evenly. "I'm a vampire. It's in the contract, hidden right down in the fine print."

His unwilling ride-share partner only shook his head, and turned away to look determinedly out the window as he said, "Like I told you, this isn't going to help anyone. The boy isn't gonna be there, and you can't do a damned thing for Manisha with the full moon coming." He glanced back at Xander with a hint of curiosity. "Assuming you even want to. What's that whole thing about, anyway? Do you two know each other or something?"

"Or something," Xander managed through a clenched jaw. "And like I mentioned before... *shut it.*"

The teenager shrugged and looked away again. Xander tried to tune out the driver's sensationalized recounting of the recent news stories about the so-called *zombie disease* in Syria. As if he didn't have enough on his plate right here in London, that shit in Damascus was going to reach a tipping point in the public consciousness one of these days, he knew. When it did, he had absolutely no clue what would happen... only that it would be Bad, with a capital *B*.

Finally, the interminable drive ended. "Nice to meet you both," the driver said pleasantly as she popped the door locks. "Have a nice day!"

Xander breathed out slowly through his nose and dragged the werewolf from the Nissan's back seat. Judging by the faded sign hanging off-kilter above the door, 314 Tedwin Mews had once been a butcher's shop. Now, it was boarded up and obviously abandoned. Clearly awaiting purchase by someone who cared enough to come and tear it down in favor of throwing up a Nando's or a KFC franchise... or something else equally horrible.

The boards sealing the front door shut had been pried free. It might have been the work of random looters, but Xander wouldn't have staked a single quid on that being the case. With the most fleeting of thoughts—quickly dismissed—that this might fall under the umbrella of actions Tré considered *reckless*, he marched his captive up to the damaged door and wrenched it open.

He could make out scuffling noises from the back of the darkened, gutted store. The noises stopped abruptly, most likely in response to the sound of the hinges on the front door shrieking. The place smelled of damp and rot. The skeletons of display shelving loomed in the shadows—some still upright, some leaning askew, and others knocked completely over, lying on the floor. At the back, a glass case ran nearly the width of the room. One end of it had been shattered, shards clinging to the frame.

As Xander's eyes adjusted, he could make out an interior door behind the counter leading to the back rooms. A sound came from beyond it. A human sound. Female. Frightened. Cut off by a lower male growl of irritation. His grip tightened on the arm of the werewolf he was holding.

"Look, mate," said the kid. "Seriously—you don't want to do this. Just turn around and walk away. It'll be better for everyone involved."

Xander didn't even bother replying. He dragged the boy forward, deeper into the store, ignoring the ghost of Tré's disapproving eyebrow looming in the back of his mind as his rage from earlier surged again. That rage was colder this time. More controlled. Which was probably a bad sign— not that he really gave a damn at the moment.

The door at the back opened onto a short hallway. There was an empty office on one side, the door hanging half off its hinges. Ahead, a pair of wider double doors gaped open, heavy and industrial looking, with darkness yawning beyond. Another werewolf stood in front of them, holding Eliz—

Holding... the woman. Manisha. His would-be damsel in distress from the club.

The male werewolf holding her was older than the wiry teenager whose arm Xander was still twisting against his back. Harder, too, by the look of it—both physically and mentally. A craggy-faced, ruddy-haired predator, even in human form. He glared at the boy in Xander's grip as they approached, rather than at Xander himself.

"What the hell, Tag?" the other werewolf asked in a low, rough voice.

Tag—who had stoically endured the best part of an hour as the hostage of a very pissed off vampire—flinched hard under the older man's angry gaze.

"Sorry. I... he..." the boy stammered.

"Your puppy gave me Fluffy's message, as instructed," Xander said, in hopes of moving things along, "but I didn't feel like cooling my heels until dusk."

"Son of a..." the older werewolf cursed under his breath.

Eliza's—*Manisha's*—eyes were pinned on Xander, wide and scared. "You came," she said, as if she couldn't quite believe it. "Please... you have to go to the warehouse. Save Sangye—"

"Quiet," her captor snapped. "You know the score, luv. You want the boy safe, you behave yourself and do as you're bid. Besides, I already told you what'll happen if you're on your own tonight, and you get loose around unsuspecting humans."

She opened her mouth as if to say something else, but the red-haired werewolf turned and shoved her hard, sending her staggering into the blackness beyond the steel doors. Xander heard her cry out as she fell, and his cold rage flared into a fiery, unthinking conflagration. He hurled Tag at his craggy faced pack-mate with inhuman strength.

The older werewolf stumbled back a step and tried to push the younger one off him, cursing viciously. But Xander had already shifted into mist, swirling past the confused tangle of limbs and re-forming. Placing himself squarely between his mate and the male who had dared to lay a hand on her. He stood, poised lightly on the balls of his feet, judging how much damage he'd have to do to put the two werewolves out of commission long enough for him to get Manisha away.

"Well," the red-haired veteran said philosophically, having righted himself on the other side of the entrance, "I s'pose that works, too."

At which point the double doors closed in Xander's face, solid and windowless, plunging the space around him into such complete darkness that even vampire eyes took a few moments to adjust.

"Erm…" he said, feeling suddenly as though he should have paid a bit more attention to the ghost of Tré's disapproving eyebrow looking down on him from above earlier.

Silence reigned for a beat, before a quiet female voice came from ground level a few feet away from him.

"It's a walk-in freezer. Crank ordered them to lock me in here for the full moon."

The depth of misery in that melodic voice pulled Xander the rest of the way back from the precipice of his unthinking fury, leaving him mired instead in a messy tangle of emotion that wavered between abject longing and utter panic.

"Are you hurt?" he asked, striving to modulate his tone into something approaching normality.

"Bruised knee, I think," she said, sounding unnaturally calm, "and my palms are scraped." Her dark silhouette—all he could make out in this lightless box of a room—eased into a seated position from the ungainly sprawl in which she'd landed. "I'm sorry," she continued. "Now you're trapped in here, too."

"I'm not the trapped one," Xander said, and scrubbed a palm over his face, trying to drag his wits out from under the avalanche of emotions that threatened to crush them into powder. "Okay, look. Here's the new plan. I'll nip outside and give those two the thrashing they so richly deserve, then come right back and get you out. Won't be two ticks."

"No, wait—" Manisha began, but Xander had already dissipated, shifting form before she could finish.

In a life as long as his, the occasional moment of abject humiliation such as this was unavoidable, but that didn't mean he wanted to wallow in it any longer than absolutely necessary. Fortunately, he thought as he circled the room, feeling for air currents, this particular abject humiliation was only a momentary detour for a vampire whose vaporous form could pass through the smallest gap.

Except... there didn't appear to be any air currents in here.

That didn't make sense, though. True, the industrial cooling units set into the wall were self-contained, recycling air that had already been cooled in the interest of efficiency, rather than bringing in warmer outside air. But even in an insulated cold room, there should be a vent tube somewhere. Otherwise, when the room's temperature went down and lowered the air pressure, it would form a vacuum that would make the doors almost impossible to open.

He let his form flow along the walls, looking for irregularities. For fuck's sake... the last thing his pride needed at this point was to have to re-form and pull up the flashlight app on his phone like some clueless wanker.

He found the air inlet on the third wall, close to the ceiling—a simple tube, little more than an inch in diameter. Still, there was no sense of air moving through it. He flowed down the tube, only to hit something soft and crumpled at the far end, where it ought to have exited the building's outer wall.

It was a wadded-up rag. Some complete *arsehole* had shoved a wadded-up rag into the only vent in the freezer.

He withdrew and let his form solidify, staring at the blank wall he could hardly make out in the dark.

Whether the werewolves had been smart and enterprising to plug the gap and make this place into a vampire prison, or whether it was as simple as the building's owner blocking the tube to keep mice and insects from getting in, the result was the same. Unless he somehow managed to batter down the heavy industrial doors, Xander was every bit as trapped as Manisha was. Trapped... with the woman he'd killed more than a hundred years ago, and whom he'd now also failed to protect from a pack of werewolves.

There was really only one reasonable response to the situation at this point.

"*Bugger*," he said, with feeling.

Six

"What's wrong?" Manisha asked. It was deeply unnerving to sit here in the dark, unable to see what was happening around her. Ever since she'd been bitten, her night vision had improved to an eerie degree, but this wasn't merely low light. It was *no* light. She brought her knees up to her chin and hugged them.

There was a rustle as the vampire trapped in the dark with her moved. When he spoke, his voice came from further away, as though he had retreated to stand as far as possible from her.

"The room's airtight. Not even mist can escape," he said in the monotone delivery of someone who was carefully locking away his reaction.

Manisha had come to understand what was behind that monotone rather intimately over the past couple of weeks. "Good," she said, in much the same tone.

He continued as though he hadn't heard her.

"Still, I suspect the lock on the doors wouldn't stand up to a sustained assault, though they might also have slid a bar through the handles to reinforce them—" He cut himself off, as if her reply had just registered. "Wait. What do you mean, *good*?"

She wrapped her arms a bit tighter around herself. "I imagine Sawbones will be guarding the entrance, at least until the full moon rises. Maybe Tag, too. If we escape, or if you attack them and they don't report in to Crank when they're supposed to, Crank will hurt Sangye to punish me."

She looked around, only uninterrupted darkness meeting her eyes, and gave a hollow laugh. It was a harsh, ugly sound. "At least the power's shut off. Otherwise, we'd both be icicles before long. This way, we just have to worry about running out of air."

"Breathing is mostly habit for vampires, rather than necessity," her companion said, still in that flat voice. "I expect what we exhale retains pretty much the same oxygen level as what we inhale. Still... I'll try to restrain myself as much as possible, as a precaution. It's no hardship, believe me—the bouquet in here leaves something to be desired."

"Yeah." The atmosphere in the stuffy, enclosed room still contained the echo of rotting meat. Manisha's stomach growled. She squeezed her eyes tightly shut, disgusted with her body's reaction.

She wondered if the vampire had heard the sound.

"If it helps, I doubt a lack of air can hurt you all that much, either," he went on. "Werewolves are notoriously difficult to kill."

Manisha swallowed. "You realize that if you're still locked in here when the moon rises tonight, I'll attack you."

"Vampires are also notoriously difficult to kill."

She shook her head, though she didn't know if he could see it. "I don't want to kill anyone. I don't want to hurt anyone." She paused. "Can you... could you do that thing where you turn into vapor? When I change, I mean? So I won't be able to do anything to you?"

Another faint rustle as he shifted position.

"If it comes to that—yes, I could." He sounded guarded. "But the better option would be for both of us to get out of here as soon as the rest of the wolves are distracted with... whatever werewolves do during the full moon."

A flash of dread made her shiver. "No. Please—you mustn't. Sawbones warned me that if I got near humans, I'd kill them. Shifting form for the first time while separated from the pack... it means I'll be maddened. Out of control. That's the punishment Crank set for my plan to meet with you secretly."

A low noise of anger emerged from the darkness.

"God... I'm going to kill that bastard if it's the last thing I do," the vampire breathed, so softly she probably wouldn't have been able to make out the words without enhanced werewolf hearing.

"Promise me right now," she insisted, needing to make him understand. "*Promise* me that you won't let me get loose around humans, and that you won't let me hurt you."

The silence stretched for a painfully long time before he replied, "I give you my word that I won't let you hurt anyone."

"Including you," she insisted.

There was a soft sound of clothing whispering against skin, as if he'd shrugged. "I'm no martyr.

Rather the opposite, in fact—and like I told you, I'm hard to damage. But we should still try to come up with an alternate plan before then."

As such things went, it was reassurance of a sort, she supposed. She scooted carefully back until she found a wall to lean against. She was exhausted, thirsty, and her head ached with a relentless dull, pounding throb. But the two of them also had quite a bit of time to pass before the moon rose the following evening.

"So," she asked, "if you're not a martyr, what are you exactly? *Who* are you?"

"You first," he countered in an arch tone. "Little Miss 'Please Help Me, My Sister was Attacked by a Vampire'."

She cringed, but refused to collapse into apologies. "Sangye is a vampire. You're a vampire. I thought playing along with Crank's plan to find you was my best chance to get help for him."

"You were being truthful about that part, then," he said evenly. "Why don't you tell me how you and the boy ended up in this mess."

Manisha took a deep breath, surprised by how much the idea of finally being able to unburden herself affected her. She let her shoulders slump, and everything she'd been holding inside poured out in a torrent of words.

Fleeing from India to London with Sangye and his retinue. The armed, black-clad police who weren't actually police. The horror of the van ride, with Sangye straining toward her in his shackles, teeth snapping mindlessly as he tried to get his jaws around her throat. Graybeard biting her. The man with the suit, smelling of death and aftershave as he told her she was *one of the vampires' whores*, and that she'd been turned into a werewolf.

"This man," her companion said, his normally velvet-lined voice gone hoarse, "did he give his name?"

"Crank called him Kovac," she said. "I guess they're still in fairly regular contact. I got the impression Crank was working for him."

A torrent of cursing foul enough to make her cheeks redden erupted from the other side of the room, only to be cut off abruptly.

"You know him, I take it?" she asked dryly, since that much was fairly obvious.

At first, she thought he might not reply. "Yes," he said eventually. "I know him. But I haven't sensed his presence, so he must not be staying in the immediate area." He seemed to shake himself free of the thought. "Okay, so you've told me who you are. Who is the boy? Royalty of some kind? Why was someone in Tezpur trying to kill him?"

Manisha hesitated for only a moment before making a leap of faith. Someone needed to know the truth, and as far as she was aware, she was the only one left who did.

"Sangye is believed by many to be the reincarnation of Tenzin Gyatso," she said, and heard the vampire inhale sharply. "Before the attack in India, he was slated for further testing by the Tibetan Lama Regent... in preparation for being confirmed as the fifteenth Dalai Lama."

Nothing moved in the silent, darkened room for a long beat.

"Please... *please* tell me you're joking," her companion said eventually.

A tiny bubble of reaction shook loose from the reservoir of hysteria lurking in Manisha's chest, making her shake.

"Why would I joke about something like that?" She pushed the hysteria back down and took a couple of deep breaths. "But the Lama Regent is dead now. Killed in the attack in Tezpur."

"The last Dalai Lama claimed before his death that he would not return," said the vampire. "He stated that the institution had served its purpose, and that he wanted to avoid political infighting with China over the process of naming a successor."

Manisha shrugged, not knowing if he could see the movement.

Her invisible companion made a frustrated noise. "He as much as said that any attempt to seat a fifteenth Dalai Lama would be a sure sign of a Chinese power play against Tibet," he continued, his voice rising. "And he died... what? Eight years ago, now? How old is the boy?"

"He died seven years ago, and Sangye is six," she said.

The sound of a body sliding down the wall to land with a soft, controlled *thump* reached her ears.

"Jesus Christ." The words were faint. "When I got near him, I remember thinking that his essence reminded me of Snag's. *Jesus tap-dancing Christ.* You're telling me... Bastian Kovac has a pack of werewolves holding the next Dalai Lama hostage... *and they've turned him into a fucking vampire."*

SEVEN

How much of a sin would it be, Xander wondered, to batter down the freezer doors, pummel whatever werewolves were lurking outside into the dirt, drag Manisha someplace far, far away, and never look back? He couldn't even begin to speculate what Kovac and his demon puppet master could do with a broken spiritual icon in the shape of a six-year-old boy.

He didn't *want* to speculate. Yet his mind tossed a hundred questions into the air. What loved one had sacrificed their life for Sangye? A parent was the most obvious answer. Xander might not have had personal experience with loving parents, but no doubt many mothers and fathers would lay down their lives without a thought to save their children.

What was Manisha's connection to the boy? How had Kovac—or Bael—even located the child in the first place? Was Kovac behind the bombing in Tezpur? If so, had he been trying to kill Sangye, or force him into the open? Why give him to a pack of werewolves? What plan did Bael have for the boy when his aim up to this point had been to destroy vampires, not add to their ranks?

The barely audible sound of ragged breathing snapped Xander away from the cascade of questions, and toward the more immediate problem that he desperately didn't want to address.

Manisha. The reincarnation of lovely, blue-eyed Eliza, who had offered him her throat for the ripping, and whose death had saved the tattered remains of his worthless soul. Saved it, and condemned it in the very same instant.

He could scent her wavering emotional control beneath the freezer's sickly-sweet smell of old meat and the unmistakable musk of wolf—still faint, since she hadn't yet seen her first full moon. If he broke out of here right now, could he possibly find and kill the wolf who had turned her in the eighteen or so hours left before moonrise?

No. It was an impossible task. Based on what she'd told him, the werewolf who turned her had been from a different pack, and packs didn't usually rub up close together. Kovac probably had him brought in from some distant, sheep-infested moor for the sole purpose of turning her, and sent him off immediately afterward.

Crank wanted to mate her, and doubtless Kovac also wanted to see that happen. The very thought made Xander's hands itch to wrap around someone's throat and squeeze until the bones snapped. But an alpha werewolf wouldn't mate someone he'd sired, directly or indirectly. Crank's pack would be made up of the wolves he'd turned, and the wolves *they'd* turned.

So Kovac had made sure Manisha was sired by an unrelated pack leader. And the odds of Xander being able to track that werewolf down in the absence of any leads was essentially nonexistent. He couldn't save her from her fate.

Quelle surprise.

Not saving people from their fates was more or less the distillation of Xander's entire existence into a nutshell.

"I've told you my story, and Sangye's," said the object of his troubled thoughts. "Now tell me yours. Who are you, and why are Crank and this Kovac person after you?"

He could hear the telltale quaver in Manisha's voice, and sensed the effort she was putting forth to try and hide it. Absolute dread over what might happen if—when—her control finally crumbled nearly strangled him. He was trapped here with her. How would he respond to the emotional breakdown of the woman who had once been Eliza?

"*Well?*" she prodded. "I think I deserve that much, at least! And it's not as though we don't have time to fill."

Xander was still sitting against the grimy wall he'd slid down earlier. He pressed the heels of his hands into his eye sockets, scrubbing at his eyes until stars burst against the backs of his eyelids. Then he let his arms fall to rest limply on his knees.

"Call me Xander," he said eventually, aware of the utter insufficiency of the answer.

And just as Eliza wouldn't have let him get away with that, neither did Manisha.

"Xander is a name, not an explanation," she said, sounding combative.

He sighed. "What else would you like to know? I'm a vampire. I'm at least half of the reason why you'll be turning into a wolf this evening. Probably more. And I'm one of the worst people you'll ever meet. The good news is, you got your first slap in preemptively. Wise choice on that, by the way. So, does that about cover it?"

"No," she said without hesitation. "It doesn't. What was that jolt I felt when our skin touched? You felt it, too—I could tell. And it's not because you're a vampire. It's never happened when I've touched Sangye."

Bloody hell, but the woman had Eliza's stubbornness in spades. He gritted his teeth.

"That jolt can most succinctly be described as 'your shitty luck.' And also, a moot point, since you're a werewolf and I'm a vampire," he said, knowing he sounded like a complete arse. Which, along with not saving the people who mattered, was *also* Xander's entire existence in a nutshell.

"Touch me again," she said, and he heard her scramble to her feet across the room. "I want to feel it properly."

"No," he said, rising as well.

Alarm jangled along his nerves. As long as he didn't touch her, he could convince himself that what he said about their connection being a moot point was true. That it didn't matter, since Xander had been too late to save her. He had failed, and now she was a werewolf. Werewolves hated vampires. Vampires hated werewolves. Q.E.D., end of story.

Because if he couldn't convince himself of that fact... if it *wasn't* a moot point and it *did* still matter, then what in the hell was he supposed to do next?

She was walking toward him blindly, one arm out in front of her to feel her way across the empty room.

"Don't," he said. He could sidestep her. Use his superior vision to stay out of her reach, or even transform into vapor again. But both of those tactics would be so completely ridiculous and pathetic that if he employed them, he'd never be able to look at himself in a mirror again.

"Why not?" she asked, her tone growing angry. "What are you afraid of? What aren't you telling me?"

With a breath of irritation at himself, he pulled out his phone and turned on the flashlight app so she could see the room properly. He propped it carefully against the base of the wall, where it would light a larger area, and straightened to face her. She was disheveled. Frightened. Wide-eyed and wild looking.

Achingly beautiful.

The polar opposite of Eliza in so many ways — deep brown eyes instead of cornflower blue, straight black hair instead of copper curls. Her frame was short and curvy instead of tall and willowy. Meanwhile, the same stubborn, kind-hearted soul gazed out from that unfamiliar olive-skinned face.

Jesus. Who was he kidding? He was fucking well *doomed*.

"Your life is complicated enough as it is," he managed with some difficulty. "Do this, and it will become about a hundred times more complicated."

Those dark eyes flashed. "Then you should have told me what I wanted to know when I asked you."

A small hand reached for him, fingers brushing the four parallel scratches on his cheek. The wounds were finally closed now, though still red and angry with slowly healing scar tissue. He caught his breath sharply as lightning shocks raced along his nerves, moving outward from the point of contact, and had to clench his jaw to avoid jerking away from the sensation that was both right, and so very, very wrong.

-o-o-o-

The fact that Manisha was expecting it this time should have made the feeling of their skin touching less shocking. It didn't, and she couldn't stop the gasp that escaped her.

It really was like touching electricity — like the time when, as a teenager, she'd stupidly tried to use a pair of needle-nosed pliers to pry the metal base of a broken light bulb out of a lamp socket without unplugging it first. She wanted to jerk away, but she *couldn't* jerk away. The sensation was grating along her nerves, putting the wolf on edge, yet the idea of *not* feeling it was somehow even worse.

And then, the visions started. Again, a confusion of images from the distant past — from other lives — assaulted her. They blotted out the here and now. Just like last time, they raced past her aware-ness so fast she couldn't grasp them individually... only to crash to a stop at a single point, which came into crystalline focus for the first time.

It was the life she had dreamed about so often. The one she'd never quite been able to remember afterward.

-o-o-o-

She stood in the massive foyer, her heavy skirts twirling around as she twisted this way and that to take in the splendor of her surroundings. The oak staircase. The crystal chandeliers. The paneled ceiling far above her head. Marble and polished wood all around, every sur-face spotless.

"Am I dreaming?" she asked, her heart pounding madly against the snug confines of her boned corset.

Strong hands closed on her shoulders from behind. Her husband turned her to face him. He was as hand-some as ever in his starched white shirt, dark waistcoat, tailored knee-length frock coat, and elegant cravat. His striking moss-green eyes met hers with their characteris-tic sharp glint of humor.

"Not dreaming," he said. "Do you like it, then? Be-cause if so, it's yours. I can have the estate agent draw up the papers later today."

Eliza couldn't help the wholly unladylike grin that stole across her face, or the excitement that leapt in her chest. She'd grown up in a single rented room with her mother and five brothers, living hand to mouth after her father had died of consumption. When she'd fallen in love with the sly-eyed and quick-witted coal merchant's son at the end of the lane, she could never have guessed that a mere ten years later, she'd be married to a man who had built up a fortune from next to nothing. She would never have believed that she'd be standing in the foyer of a fashionable London mansion that was hers for the asking.

She'd started life as a destitute flower girl, and ended up the wife of a powerful mill owner who made more money in the space of a single month than she had expected to see cumulatively during her lifetime. She had so many plans now; so many dreams. There was so much she could do that she would never have been able to do before.

There was the women's suffrage movement. Prison reform. The Labouchere Amendment. She wanted to make a difference with all of it. To use her newfound wealth to help others. But would it be so terribly bad if she also lived in a beautiful house while she did those things?

She realized she was holding her breath. The low voice in her ear made her shiver deliciously, as it always did.

"We can afford it Eliza. I promise you. You'll still be able to slay your dragons. Besides, all those stuffy lords and ladies you'll be entertaining will take you a lot more seriously when your footmen show them into a fine drawing room, and the butler serves them expensive port."

There was a reason her husband had been able to build an empire out of a handful of farthings. It was because he was both terrifyingly intelligent and terrifyingly shrewd. He also had an annoying penchant for being right about things.

"I love it, Alexander," she said. "Please have the estate agent finalize the sale as soon as possible, so we can move in."

-o-o-o-

Green eyes closed against her touch as if in pain. That sharply handsome, eerily familiar face tipped to the side as the vampire leaned away from her fingers, breaking the contact between them.

She caught her breath as something slotted neatly into place inside her mind.

"Alexander Charles Grimshaw," she whispered. "You're him."

The vampire melted back into the shadows, beyond the reach of the arc of white light and dust motes that cut through the room.

"Alexander Grimshaw died well over a hundred years ago," he said. "Do yourself a favor. Don't try to remember him, and for god's sake don't mourn him."

"Oh. Oh, I see now! The man who captured me. Kovac," she continued, oblivious to his words. "He called me 'one of the vampires' whores.' In one of my past lives, I was your wife."

"Argh. Fucking *Buddhists*," he growled. "You could at least have the decency to sound shocked."

She shook her head, slowly lowering her hand from where it still hung in the air, suspended. "Why? Reincarnation is just a part of life. There's a whole industry in my homeland devoted to tracking down the reincarnations of people's loved ones. Look at me—I'm pledged to serve a child who is probably the next Dalai Lama."

"Except for the small point about him being a vampire now, and you being a werewolf," he said brutally.

A chill flowed down the length of her spine at the reminder of what awaited her this evening when the moon rose.

"So, is that what causes the shock when we touch?" she asked, trying to focus on the present instead. "The fact that we were connected in another life?"

"No," he said, still cloaking his features in the darkness.

"What, then?" she asked, frowning.

Silence. Until—

"You know, I'm not sure which would make me more of a bastard. Telling you now, or waiting for you to remember it on your own."

Manisha was generally a patient woman. But the restless beast inside her was eating away at her composure, its presence becoming harder and harder to ignore.

"Fine," she snapped. "You don't think I deserve a full explanation for everything that's been done to me over the past few weeks? Then get back over here so I can touch you again, and I'll bloody well figure it out for myself."

The shadows in the corner moved as he shifted uneasily in place.

She clenched her fists, feeling her control unraveling moment by moment. "I am scared out of my wits right now," she forced out, feeling the telltale burn of tears at the backs of her eyes. "I'm about to become a monster, and for all I know, a six-year-old boy is undergoing torture right now as some sort of twisted punishment for my actions. I'm trapped with a man from a past life who won't talk to me, I feel sick and weak and dizzy, and *I don't know what to do now.*"

A harsh breath came from the shadows, and that sharp-eyed face from the distant past emerged once more into the pale slash of light.

"I can't save you, Manisha," he said. "I'm the very last person you should come to for that."

She stared at him, seeing old pain looking back at her rather than the seamless armor he'd presented earlier.

"I think that may be the first truly honest thing you've said to me," she told him. A long breath escaped her. "It's all right. I'm beyond saving. I know that. What about Sangye, though?"

He swallowed, the shadow of his Adam's apple bobbing in the odd lighting from the mobile phone. "No one can undo what's been done to him."

"But will you get him away from Crank? From Kovac? Will you try to get him to safety?"

He paused as if choosing his words carefully. Manisha wished he would stop doing that. "I'm not sure there's such a thing as safety for any of us, now. I have allies, though. I've told them about the boy, and where he's currently being held. They will try to help him. Which reminds me…"

He picked up his phone and unlocked it, his rapid typing making the LED on the back waver crazily.

"What are you doing?"

"Texting them this address, so they'll have the information when they arrive. Unfortunately, they won't get here in time to do much for us tonight," he said. The flashlight app flicked off, plunging them into darkness again. "Sorry, but I need to conserve the battery."

"Don't worry about it," she said, even though the disorientation of the uninterrupted blackness made her already queasy stomach feel even worse. "So, your friends. They're also vampires? And they're coming here?"

"Yes, and yes," he said. "The ones who aren't halfway around the world are coming here, at any rate."

"Okay." That didn't do much to ease her immediate worries about what might be happening to Sangye, but at least other people with motivation to help him knew about his existence and location. If something happened to her and Alexander—or Xander, rather—maybe there would still be hope for him.

A new wave of dizziness made her waver on her feet. A hand appeared on her upper arm, steadying her, the thrum of power between them muted by the worn material of her jacket. She widened her stance, but her knees still trembled, threatening to give out.

"I… uh… really don't feel at all well," she said weakly. "Is that because of the full moon coming on?"

Xander's grip tightened. "I'm not sure. Probably." He urged her a few steps backward, until her back met one of the grimy, insulated wall panels.

"Sit down. Try to get some rest. Maybe even some sleep. I expect you'll need it later." The last few words were grim.

She let him guide her down to sit on the floor with her back braced against the wall, as she had been earlier. She noticed that he was very careful not to let their bare skin touch, and that he retreated across the room again once she was settled.

"What's going to happen to me tonight?" she whispered. "I mean, exactly?"

"I can't answer that question," he said. "I've seen werewolves in human form, and I've seen werewolves in wolf form. I've never seen what happens in between the two forms."

She digested that for a moment. "You can transform yourself, though. What's it like for you? Does it hurt?"

"No," he said immediately. "No, it doesn't hurt. It was difficult to master at first, but now it comes quite naturally."

"Maybe it's natural and easy for werewolves, too," she said.

Inside her, the wolf growled and pushed against its restraints, impatient.

EIGHT

Xander let the silence stretch, unwilling to offer empty reassurance beyond what he'd already given her. If her transformation were going to be easy, Crank wouldn't have ordered her locked up in here as a form of punishment. Sawbones wouldn't have warned her about killing humans, and he also wouldn't have evinced such satisfaction at trapping Xander in here with her.

That works, too, the red-haired werewolf had said in a philosophical tone as he slammed the door closed on them. There appeared to be little question that the other werewolves expected things inside their makeshift prison to turn ugly.

Buried rage at everything he was powerless to change was becoming so much a part of him these days that its resurgence was almost like the return of an old friend. Xander knew that fact should probably scare the ever-living fuck out of him. The problem was, it was usually easier to deal with the rage than to deal with the alternative.

He watched Manisha's dark silhouette as she removed her jacket and wadded it up to use as a rough pillow. Evidently, she intended to take his glib advice about getting some rest to heart. It worried him that she was already feeling ill with so many hours still to wait before moonrise.

"I don't know if I can sleep," she said, sounding thoroughly wretched.

It seemed that all of his quips, all of his wisecracks and smart-ass remarks had deserted him without a trace. "Try," he told her, in the absence of anything else to offer.

Silence fell again, and within a few minutes her breathing had evened out into sleep despite her protestations. He wished he could take even partial credit for that. The next twenty-four hours would look completely different if he could affect her mind with his mental powers. But, of course, he'd tried the moment she'd come toward him with her hand raised to touch him. His mental suggestion had no effect. Hell, there was no indication she'd even noticed the attempt.

They were both dark creatures, and his darkness held no sway over hers. He settled back in the corner and listened to her breathe.

The hours passed, broken only by Manisha's occasional restlessness. She was asleep again when his phone vibrated with a new text from Tré. It stated that he'd received the address of the old butcher's shop, but the five of them were delayed in Athens. Their new ETA would barely get them to Heathrow before the sun came up tomorrow. Which meant Xander couldn't expect the cavalry to charge in until the following dusk, at the earliest. Not unless he wanted the cavalry in question to arrive crispy-frittered from the sun.

He texted back his understanding and warned Tré that he would be powering his phone off to save the twenty-two percent of the battery he presently had left. Then, he leaned back against the wall and settled in to wait.

Hours passed.

Manisha's sleep was restless. Xander tried very hard not to speculate about the contents of her dreams. He judged that it must be late morning when the rhythm of her breathing changed from slumber to wakefulness. She didn't move or speak for several moments.

When she finally did, it was to say, "*Ah,*" in the tone of someone who had just experienced a revelation. He tensed, waiting for the rest.

"I get it now," she said. Her voice was gravelly from sleep and lack of water. "We were married, but now you're a vampire and you look about the same age as you did back then. You killed me when you were turned, didn't you? Like Sangye killed his mother."

"What makes you assume that?" he asked, trying to postpone the inevitable.

"Is it true?" she countered.

"Yes. It's true," he said. "You looked up at me with those big blue eyes, told me that you trusted me completely, and I ripped your throat out with my teeth. I still remember the look of surprise on your face as you died. I remember it, and then I do my best to get so hammered that I can't remember my own name, much less yours. Easier said than done for a vampire."

She pondered that for a moment.

"That explains... quite a bit, really," she said, her tone musing.

He raised an eyebrow she couldn't see. "I did say you were smart to get your first slap in preemptively." She was silent for a bit. The pause ate at him. "No additional commentary to offer on what I just told you?" he couldn't help asking.

"What sort of commentary are you expecting?" she asked.

He crossed his arms, still hunched in the farthest corner from her. "The correct response is to express anger, and/or fear, and/or horror at the prospect of being trapped in a walk-in freezer with the man who brutally murdered you more than a century ago. Unless this is some kind of a werewolf thing?"

"Some kind of... werewolf thing?" This time, he could hear the faint bewilderment in her voice. "What are you talking about?"

He freed one hand to wave it in a frustrated gesture that encompassed her unnatural air of detachment. Of course, she couldn't see that, either. "The whole eerily calm and politely interested thing. You're supposed to be afraid now."

Even the beat of silence before she spoke sounded bemused. "I'm trapped in a freezer and I'm going to turn into a werewolf in a few hours. I'm bloody *terrified*. Is that not coming across? I thought I'd been pretty up-front about it."

"You're supposed to be afraid *of me* now," he clarified, unsure why he felt the need to belabor the issue to this degree.

"Oh," she said. "Right. Look... I'm sorry, but as things stand right now, you're pretty far down my list of concerns. I mean—I was stuck in the back of a van with Sangye right after he was turned into a vampire. If the chains he was shackled with had been a few centimeters longer, or if one of the bolts holding them had snapped, it's pretty clear he would have ripped me apart without batting an eyelash. But then by the next day, he was better — more or less back to his old self. Am I supposed to hold that van ride against him?"

Xander closed his eyes, wishing he could just rewind the last few minutes and not be having this conversation. "No. But... he didn't *actually hurt you*."

"I don't think that's really the point." He could hear the frustration creeping into her voice; hear the slow breath she took to try and contain it. "If becoming a vampire turns the *Dalai Lama* into a murderous ball of bloodlust, I think one can safely assume that it would turn *anyone* into a murderous ball of bloodlust. So unless you purposely sought out vampirism, knowing what it would entail — "

"*I didn't ask for any of this!*" he nearly shouted, only to clamp his jaw shut in horror against the torrent of enraged pain that suddenly tried to tear its way out of his chest.

This. *This* was why he didn't let anything real slip out from behind his facade without first wrapping it in a muffling blanket of sarcasm and defensive humor. He stood frozen in his corner, listening to the echoes fade.

"No," Manisha said evenly. "I didn't think you had."

And this was the part where he opened his mouth and apologized for being an arse. Except that the breath was locked in his chest; his lips and tongue lying paralyzed and useless.

"I'm going to try to sleep more," Manisha said. "I still feel really sick and weak."

"Yes. Good idea. You do that," he whispered. "I'll keep watch."

-o-o-o-

Sleeping—or, at least, dozing—worked until late afternoon. Time was meaningless inside the light-less box she shared with a bitter and wounded man whom she had once loved in another life. Time *should* have been meaningless, anyway—but the wolf knew that the full moon was coming, whether it could see the progress of the sun across the sky or not.

Restlessness eventually drew her to unsteady feet, and she paced the small space on wobbling knees. She felt like throwing up, but for one thing, doing so would only dehydrate her more, and for another, she didn't really want to have to navigate around a puddle of sick in the dark. Chills wracked her, which was ridiculous since the disused freezer had grown sweltering over the course of the last sixteen-plus hours.

"Is there anything I can do?" Xander asked quietly, without moving from his spot in the corner.

Part of her wanted to curl up in his arms and listen to that rich, velvet voice while he stroked her hair and told her that everything would be all right. The other part wanted to attack him and tear him into tiny pieces. The conflicting impulses infuriated her. She paused in her pacing, realizing that she was scratching her bare forearms hard enough to bloody them.

"I think you should change into mist now," she said, striving to keep the confusing tangle of neediness and anger out of her tone.

"It's still more than half an hour until moonrise," he said. "There's a bit of time left."

"That may be," she grated, "but I'm fighting a very strong urge to hit you right now."

He shifted position in the dark. "Don't feel bad. I'm told that's quite a common reaction to spending more than an hour or two at a time in my presence."

Her temper snapped. "*Is everything a joke to you? Do you have any idea how much it scares me that I might hurt someone? Hurt you?*"

"No, and yes," he said, his voice growing intense. "I killed you, remember? I know *exactly* what it feels like to come back to yourself with the blood of a loved one dripping down your chin."

"*So change!*" she yelled, and lunged toward the space where she thought he was standing. Strong hands caught her, ignoring the way her fingers clasped around his biceps like claws, nails digging into the fabric of his expensive shirt.

"I will," he promised, "when it's time."

Wolf and woman wavered between aggression and surrender for a breathless moment before she crumpled into him, feeling the low vibration of energy thrumming between them. It wasn't really an embrace, but he supported her as she shuddered against him, eyes wide open and dry of tears.

"I can't do this," she whispered. "I can't do this. *I can't do this.*"

The grip on her arms tightened. "I don't think it's something you do, Manisha," he said. Her cheek rested against him, and she rolled her head to press her ear to his chest and feel the rumble as he finished, "It just *is*, and you do your best to let it happen without fighting it."

They stayed like that for what seemed like an age, unmoving and unspeaking. The grating restlessness inside her grew into a physical ache, until her bones felt like they were covered in sandpaper, rasping against the muscles and sinews. She whimpered.

"It's almost moonrise," Xander said reluctantly.

"Please go," Manisha said, hating the quiver in her voice. "Change, I mean. Get away from me."

Stupidly, she was still clutching his arms even as she told him to leave her. Slick wetness coated her fingertips, and she realized with a lurch of her stomach that her fingernails had lengthened into claws and pierced his skin. The smell of blood tickled her nostrils. The wolf pricked up, scenting the air.

"*Namo Buddhaya!*" she cursed, wrenching her hands away. "Go. *Go!*"

He hesitated, but then said, "I'll be right here. Even if you can't see me—I'm here. It's just one night, Manisha. A single night, and then it's over."

Until the next full moon, she thought miserably. But she only nodded, the bones in her neck popping and crackling painfully.

The callused hands holding her did not fall away. They dissolved, and the sense of a solid body in front of her in the darkness disappeared between one breath and the next. A sharp pain rippled down the length of her spine, dropping her to her hands and knees. Panic sent her heart racing.

Agony spread from her gut outward, muscles seizing and tearing, bones and joints twisting impossibly. Manisha threw her head back and screamed until she thought her lungs would explode.

NINE

Manisha's scream of mortal agony echoed around the enclosed space, warping and echoing until it became a wolf's howl. The sonic vibrations danced through the space Xander occupied near the ceiling of the freezer, reflecting off the walls and buffeting him with an aria of tormented misery.

In this form, his physical senses were nearly useless, but his mental senses expanded to compensate. He wasn't sure if that was better or worse. He was aware of Manisha—of the wolf—twitching on the floor like a creature in its death throes. Instead of stilling though, the movements became more violent as time went on, her unfamiliar new body fighting to gain control of itself.

Within minutes, she was attempting to gain her feet, only to fall back to the ground over and over. Eventually, she stood braced on forepaws splayed widely apart, hind legs scrambling on the slick floor. She was a pack animal, trapped alone and at her most vulnerable, and Xander didn't need to be able to smell her panic in order to sense it.

Within an hour, the wolf was walking... prowling with stumbling steps around the square box in which she was trapped. Within two hours, her sniffing at corners became scrabbling, became whimpering, became howling, as her desperation to escape rose in tandem with the strength and co-ordination of her muscles.

By the third hour, she was hurling herself at the seam between the double doors, ripping at it with her claws. Xander wasn't entirely sure the doors would hold, nor was he entirely sure what to do if they didn't, given his glib promise earlier not to let her hurt any innocents.

The doors held.

There was no way to tell for certain, but he thought it must be nearing midnight when her de-meanor changed again. The rage and fear that had been turned outward toward her prison suddenly focused inward. Like a rabid dog, Manisha turned on herself, teeth snapping and tearing at her own flanks. Yips and howls of pain rent the air. Mad-ness permeated the small space like a sickly pall.

She tore at herself until she collapsed with ex-haustion, only to stagger upright after a few minutes and do it all over again... over and over and over.

Xander hovered on the cusp of materializing and taking his chances at physically restraining her, only the knowledge that his corporeal presence would madden her further holding him back. He didn't know how strong she was, but the dents and gouges deforming the steel doors' interior surface spoke of strength no natural wolf would possess.

The odds were that he would not be able to re-strain her—not without injuring her at least as badly as she was injuring herself. In fact, the odds were that they would both end up injured. But the morning would eventually come, bringing new dangers for both of them. He, at least, needed to try and be ready for what would come... afterward.

So Xander hovered throughout the night, as the soul of the woman he'd loved more than life or power or money shrieked in terrified agony. Inside him, the rage that had bubbled and simmered for more than a hundred years solidified into a solid mass that demanded its day of revenge. Revenge on Bael. On Bastian Kovac. On the wolves who dared touch his mate—who had dared even *look* at her. At that moment, Xander would gladly have tortured every goddamn one of them for the rest of his days.

He *hated*, like he'd never before hated in his long, miserable life.

No night had ever been as interminable as this one, he was certain.

When Manisha collapsed for the last time, her animal form shuddering and seizing as her limbs lengthened and her hide changed from thick fur to a smooth, naked, *human* expanse of skin, Xander rematerialized, feeling as exhausted as though he'd been the one fighting all night.

He immediately started tugging the buttons of his shirt free with shaking fingers. Manisha's clothing lay scattered in useless shreds around the dark room. He paused only long enough to power up his phone and turn on its light, propping it against the wall again so he could better assess the damage she'd done to herself.

Christ. Her sides were bruised and bleeding, torn by sharp teeth. Her skin was deathly pale, a gray cast beneath its usual olive-brown. He pulled off his shirt, intending to use it to cover her, and fell to his knees at her side. She was facedown, arms splayed and one leg hitched up to the side.

"Manisha." His voice was hoarse as he reached down to place a hand on her shoulder. "It's over now. It's *over*."

His fingertips closed around her warm flesh, and he was knocked on his arse the next instant as she exploded into motion, her eyes glowing yellow and her lips pulled back to reveal jagged teeth.

"Fucking *hell*—" Xander's curse was cut off when inhumanly strong hands closed around his throat and he was slammed onto his back on the gritty floor. He stared up at a figure whose body might have regained its usual shape, but whose mind was still caught between human and beast.

Shock immobilized him for the space of a heartbeat before he jammed a knee between their bodies and tried to buck her off without accidentally hurting her further. It was about as effective as trying to remove an industrial magnet from a steel beam with his fingernails. He gritted his teeth and pushed sideways instead. They grappled with each other, rolling around as they fought for dominance.

A crunch of glass came from beneath his shoulder as he slammed against the base of the wall. The LED on the phone flickered out, plunging them back into darkness. They rolled over again and Xander finally gained the upper hand, trapping Manisha beneath him.

She still hadn't released her grip on his throat. Unless she actually twisted his head *off*, she couldn't kill him by strangling him, but even after more than a century of functional immortality, his body still fought instinctive panic at the feeling of thumbs crushing his trachea.

He used his larger frame to pin her in place so he could rip her hands away, only to feel razor sharp teeth tear into his left forearm as he did so. The resulting curse lodged in his injured throat, which was already knitting itself back together while Manisha did her best to rip into whatever other parts of him she could reach. Xander tried to get a better angle to restrain her more fully, but she just used the moment to wriggle free like an eel and tackle him once more.

Teeth closed on the muscle running from his neck to his shoulder. He felt his fangs lengthen and his eyes burn with a vampiric glow, the darkness inside him rising in response to the attack by another dark creature. Manisha shook her head violently from side to side, tearing at his flesh. Blood ran down his arm in rivulets, and every higher brain function he still possessed shut down between one breath and the next. He hissed, plunging headfirst into a terrible, roiling swirl of mingled frustration and bloodlust.

Emphasis — god help him — on the *lust.*

Because Manisha was also grinding her body against his as she tore into him. And... well... he wasn't really making any concerted attempt to stop her. No — one of his hands was gripping her hip hard enough to bruise, while the other tangled in her heavy, dark hair and used the hold to jerk her head to the side. As his fangs sank into her neck, he tried to tell himself it was in the hopes that draining her blood would weaken her enough for them both to *calm the fuck down* for a minute—because if she kept doing what she was doing he was in real danger of coming in his pants like a goddamned teenager.

Xander made no bones about the fact that he'd done some seriously fucked-up shit in the last hundred and twenty years. Drinking werewolf blood while the werewolf in question dry-humped him into the concrete floor of a locked walk-in freezer arguably topped that list. But for some reason, the ever-present smell of wet dog no longer mattered. The fact that both of them were now bleeding freely from multiple wounds didn't matter. Nor did the fact that their guards might return and fling open the doors at any moment.

He knew the rather strange, dizzy sensation creeping over him as he swallowed mouthful after mouthful of Manisha's werewolf blood should be a giant red flag that this maybe wasn't the smartest idea he'd ever had. But Manisha's hands had stopped digging ragged furrows across his chest and ribcage in favor of ripping open his fly, and the only red he could see right now was the blood smeared across her naked body.

All right—that was actually a lie. There was also the red haze wafting across his vision as she grabbed his rock hard, aching cock and impaled herself on it, crying out in what might have been pain, pleasure, or both.

Xander growled against the flesh of her neck and thrust up into her blazing heat, no more able to stop himself than he could stop the tide or the orbital motion of the planets. His head was swimming. He released her throat with a gasp, letting his skull fall back with a solid thump against the floor. A predator's teeth sank into the flesh beneath his collarbone, which might have pissed him off rather a lot if she hadn't twisted her hips *just so* at the same time.

"*Fuck*," he groaned, and dragged her off him with a sudden burst of strength.

This was supposed to be the part where he pushed her away; put some distance between them and tried to reason with her. Tried to coax her humanity back to the forefront. Instead, he wrestled her down and flipped her over onto her knees so he could enter her from behind. She keened and pushed her hips back to take him as deep as possible, drawing a rumbling growl from the depths of his chest that was utterly beyond his control.

Xander slammed into her, and she met him thrust for thrust, her cries growing into screams until her inner muscles clamped around his dick and she jerked out her climax, nearly sobbing with the strength of it. Xander had no room to comment — the noise he made as he followed her over the edge was not precisely what one would call *dignified*. The sensation was so intense that he suspected his vision had gone black, though in the lightless room there was no way to independently confirm the suspicion.

When the excruciating pleasure finally loosed its grip, he realized that the dizziness had grown exponentially worse in the interim. Manisha might have been feeling the same effects, because they collapsed to the side together in slow motion, panting hard in the stale air of the enclosed freezer. He slipped out of her warm body and shivered, flopping over to lie spread-eagled on his back as the room spun around him. Rational thought was still out of reach, but the vague feeling of having just done something hopelessly, *monumentally* stupid was creeping over his awareness, nonetheless.

"What—" she rasped, sounding fully human once more.

"... just happened?" he finished, staring blankly at the slowly spinning blackness above him.

Awkward didn't begin to describe the silence that followed.

"I feel really, *really* strange," she whispered hoarsely.

"Uh-huh," he agreed. "I'm right there with you, love."

Of course, that was the cue for one of the double doors to creak open, spilling a thin rectangle of weak light into the room. He and Manisha had fetched up in one of the far corners, and the illumination did not reach them.

"One of my men trapped the vampire in here with her." It was Fluffy, his voice sounding as though it were reaching Xander through a tunnel. "He'll be dead by now. She will have torn him to pieces during the blood rage. You want me to take her back to the warehouse and put her in with the boy again? He still won't feed from the humans we put in his cell."

The sense of a horribly familiar and unwelcome presence washed over Xander's reeling senses, even before a voice answered in a deep Eastern European drawl.

"Yes, yes. Do whatever it takes to make him feed," Bastian Kovac said carelessly. "The whelp is of no use to me if he's in a coma."

The double doors opened the rest of the way, illuminating the freezer's interior and silhouetting the two figures standing in the entrance.

"*Kovac.*" Rage drove Xander to his feet, but it was not enough to sustain him against the frightening sickness draining his strength. He took a single, staggering step and collapsed back to the floor.

Kovac peered down his nose at Xander. His image blurred, two more Kovacs appearing on either side of the original one, sliding in and out of focus for a moment before they merged back into a single figure.

"Dead, you say?" Kovac said with a sneer. "You're an idiot, Crank."

Crank shoved past him to stare down at Xander and Manisha. Xander saw the werewolf's eyes move from his bare chest to his ripped trousers. Saw his nostrils flare. The room reeked of sex and blood. He probably didn't even need werewolf senses to smell it.

"You might've knocked first, Fluffy," he slurred. "Is there no respect for people's privacy anymore?"

Even with his vision going dim and fuzzy again, Xander took a moment to relish the look of wide-eyed, apoplectic rage on Fluffy's face as he put two and two together.

"Tag! Sawbones!" the alpha roared. "Bring silver chains for the bitch, and iron for the bloodsucker!" He stepped closer, standing over Xander like an enraged pit bull. "I will fucking well make you suffer for this before you die."

Manisha lay unresponsive next to him—possibly out cold. Never mind the danger to himself—Xander knew that the potential danger to his mate made this the worst possible time to lose his tenuous hold on consciousness. Unfortunately, that didn't stop the whirling dizziness from stealing the last remnant of his sight, hearing, and rational thought, leaving him in comfortable darkness.

TEN

Cold metal encircled Xander's wrists, ankles and neck when he next regained awareness. Gashes and bite marks covered his upper body; many of them still open and bleeding sluggishly. The vertigo hadn't gone away, either; now, it threatened to make his gorge rise. He moved one arm from its uncomfortable twisted position, and it took a shocking amount of effort to do so. The iron shackle burning his skin with its metallic chill wasn't *that* heavy, surely.

Chains clanked with his ungainly attempt, and the movement of his arm was halted abruptly as the slack ran out. He swallowed, his dry throat clicking.

Manisha. She was in danger. He had to get to her. He *had* to —

With far too much difficulty, he peeled sticky eyelids open to reveal a fuzzy swirl of color that spun in lazy, nauseating circles around him.

The chains. Focus on the chains. He had to get out of them. Until he did that, he wasn't going anywhere.

Escape should have been a matter of such insignificance as to hardly be worth mentioning. A moment's thought, an application of will, and he would swirl away in a cloud of vapor. Hell, even the owl could slip free of them, though the heavy iron band around his neck might do some damage to delicate avian bones if he wasn't careful. He reached inward, attempting to gather the power at his center.

Nothing.

No rush of dematerialization. No clang of metal on concrete as the restraints fell free. He tried again. No flurry of wings and feathers followed.

Fuck.

He'd shifted form in the past while more seriously injured than this, he was certain. And yet, he couldn't remember ever feeling quite like he did right now, despite all the questionable things he'd imbibed through the medium of human blood during the course of his lifetime. He blinked rapidly, forcing his gritty eyes into something approaching focus.

The dizziness was disorientating, but his vision cleared enough for him to get a better idea of his surroundings. A moment later, he wished it hadn't. He was shackled to a heavy steel bike rack sunk into the pavement on which he was sprawled. Multi-story buildings crowded both sides of the narrow, deserted roadway. Plywood and boards covered fully half of the windows in his field of view. The whole area looked derelict.

And it was daylight.

His position at the edge of the pavement was still in shadow, but this was not the soft light of breaking dawn. It was the light of mid-morning. He squinted at the edge of the weak London sunlight illuminating the roadway, trying to force his vision to stop wavering. He stared fixedly at it for several moments, long enough to confirm that the edge of the shadow was, in fact, creeping inexorably toward him. He let his eyes slip closed and gritted his teeth, straining once more to force his body into transformation.

"*Bloody... buggering...*" he grated, and jerked at the chains, the movement as weak as a kitten's. "Son of a poxy whore!"

For the first time, real panic nibbled at the edges of his composure. He couldn't be trapped here like an ant under a sadistic child's magnifying glass, helpless and impotent and *useless* as the sunlight crept across the tarmac. Not when Manisha needed him.

"Hello!" he called, his voice raspy and not nearly as loud as he would have liked. "*Hello*! Is anyone about?"

There was no answer. And even if there had been... even if some human had come to investigate and he'd been able to mentally influence them, what did he expect them to do? Unless they just happened to be carrying around a heavy-duty hacksaw or a set of lock-picks, no human was going to be able to get him free of these damned chains.

"*Shite!*" he practically roared, and then collapsed into an undignified coughing fit as the shout dragged sandpaper over his parched throat.

He eyed the creeping sunlight again, trying to determine how much of its movement was due to the rising sun, and how much due to his swimming vision. What would the authorities make of it when someone eventually found him? As far as anyone knew, no vampire had ever been killed by sunlight... though all of them had been injured by it to various degrees at one point or another. And they all agreed that the sun's caress was just about the most painful sensation a vampire seemed capable of experiencing.

Would he be left as a burned corpse, or would the sun consume even his bones, leaving nothing behind but a smear of dust and ash? How much of the process would he have to experience in brilliant Technicolor before he lost consciousness?

And why couldn't he fucking *move*, or at least think properly? What the hell was wrong with him? Was Manisha suffering the same effects? It had seemed earlier that she might be, when Fluffy and that rotting stain on humanity Bastian Kovac had shown up.

Jesus... *Manisha*. He growled in frustration and tried to jerk against the chains again, but the effort only made gray fog swirl across his unsteady vision. When it cleared enough to see once more, the line of sunlight had jumped forward and was now only a few inches from his feet. He dragged his legs closer to his body and called out again, but this area was clearly deserted—a forgotten corner of the city that had been abandoned and left to rot as London's economy plummeted.

Twice more, he struggled against the chains until consciousness wavered, and when he came back to himself, the light was closer. He'd already shuffled around until he was as far into the dwindling shadows as the chains would allow, his limbs twisted uncomfortably.

Now, the shadow's edge lay perhaps two inches from his fingertips. He clenched the hand into a fist and closed his eyes, trying to center himself enough to reach out mentally. The others would be here in London by now, unless something else had detained them. Safely holed up someplace with a roof, presumably, and unable to venture forth in the daylight to help him even if they knew where he was—which they didn't.

Hell, who did he think he was kidding? *Xander* didn't even know where he was.

But if they were within mental range, he could at least tell them goodbye, and beg them to help Manisha and Sangye. He might not know where *he* was, but it had sounded like they were taking Manisha back to the warehouse in Battersea.

Perhaps unsurprisingly, focus was elusive. Xander thought he sensed the others as distant presences, but he could not solidify the connection. Even that small comfort was to be denied to him, it seemed.

It was probably for the best, he tried to tell himself. There was no telling how long he'd be able to maintain his mental shields. And while Xander was a selfish bastard and always had been, he wasn't selfish enough to force the others to experience his excruciating death vicariously.

I'm so sorry, Manisha, he thought. *I did warn you that I was the last person you should look to for salvation.*

He stared at his hand with eyes that slid in and out of focus. There was one final decision to be made, it seemed. Should he continue to cower here in the building's disappearing shade while the slow march of sunlight incinerated him an inch at a time? Or should he hurl himself into its path and be done with it faster?

He wavered, watching the sunlight close the final fraction of space to his balled-up hand. When he tried to tense his muscles, he discovered it was a moot point. He didn't have the strength to move. Trembling, breath trapped in his lungs, he lay there as the golden sunlight slid over his clenched knuckles.

Nothing happened.

He blinked.

Nothing continued to happen.

The light crept over his hand, warming the skin with a long-forgotten sensation that he had never thought to experience again. It slid over his wrist and up his forearm with a lover's silken caress, illuminating his deathly pale skin under a faint glow. He retraced its path upwards, to the fiery orb peeking over the rooftops, wishing his damned dizziness would subside enough for the sky to stop spinning.

"Huh. All right, then. Have to say, I really didn't see that one coming," he mumbled to no one in particular before promptly passing out like a snuffed candle, his body finally giving up the fight against the creeping weakness that dragged him down into blackness.

ELEVEN

Manisha experienced the trip back to the warehouse in Battersea as a series of disconnected snippets.

One moment, she was being dragged like a sack of grain between two large figures, something hard and cold burning into the skin of her wrists.

Then, she was in the back of a lorry, her battered and exhausted body jouncing with every bump in the road.

Time jumped, and Sawbones was looking down at her, an expression of displeasure or distaste twisting his craggy features as double vision made him waver in and out of focus.

Another jump. She was being manhandled again, her bare feet scraping painfully against the gritty pavement as the rust-stained white walls of the warehouse loomed ahead of her.

The next thing she knew, she was back in the familiar cell, lying on the floor, too weak to even sit up. A bucket of water splashed across her face and upper body, shockingly cold against her naked skin. She couldn't even raise the energy to splutter. She just laid there, muscles quaking with cold and weakness, and stared blankly at the blurry figures in front of her and the open cell door beyond.

"She's no use to anyone right now," said a disgusted voice. "Leave her to sleep it off for a few hours and try again."

Her arms were roughly dragged around, the cold metal around her wrists searing her skin a little deeper. Chains clinked, feet stepped over her, and a moment later the door slammed shut. She lay there—cold, exposed, and helpless—and tried to understand what had happened to her.

"Are you there, Kumari Sadhu?" came a quiet voice from the other side of the thick wall. "Please. Please answer me."

She worked her throat, trying to swallow enough saliva to moisten it.

"I'm here," she said hoarsely, unsure if he'd be able to hear her. "It's all right, Sangye."

Of course, that was a lie. Nothing was all right, and she didn't know if it would ever be all right again. Bits and pieces of the past night and morning were started to organize themselves within her mind—a scattered jigsaw of memory, nightmare, and fevered imagining.

She was a werewolf. She had turned into a raging beast, and it had been horrific. Pure torment. Her wolf had been terrified. Desperate to get free — to escape the trap of the freezer and find its pack. To run. To hunt. To be with others of its kind.

She remembered the feeling as terror had given way to madness. The wolf wanted to rend flesh, and the only flesh within reach had been hers. Thank all that was holy Xander had agreed to stay out of her reach. She would have killed him—or killed herself in the attempt.

She'd thought at first that maybe her memory of what had happened next was a hallucination. For one thing, Xander's voice as he'd tried to comfort her had sounded completely different from its usual cold drawl.

Manisha, he'd said, his tone like roughened velvet. *It's over now. It's over.*

His callused fingers had felt so cool on her sweat-soaked, overheated skin. Her wolf had wanted to pounce on him—to try to make him yield, and see if he was strong enough to make her submit to him instead. Her heart pounded faster in a twisted tangle of shame and excitement as she remembered grabbing him by the throat... rubbing against him intimately... tearing at the maddening fabric that stood between her and the enticing expanse of cool flesh the she wanted so badly. That she *needed*.

Some tiny human part of her had been appalled by what was happening. She was *horrified* at herself. What she was doing was illegal. Immoral. Indefensible. Physical and sexual assault—two of the worst crimes one human being could perpetrate against another. But... neither of them was human anymore.

Still, she cringed as she remembered the way she'd practically *wallowed* in his blood. Some of it was still on her skin, for crying out loud, just as her blood was probably still on his.

He hadn't reacted with fear or horror at what she was doing, though. He hadn't even reacted with anger. At least, not exactly. No, he'd risen to the wolf's challenge, taken control, and given Manisha and her wolf exactly what they'd needed. The twin fang marks on the side of her neck throbbed with a deep, aching heat that echoed another part of her body that he had pierced. That heat helped drive back the awful chill of her wet skin against the bare, cold floor of the cell.

Manisha was far from being a blushing virgin, but the memory of what she and Xander had done to each other did bring a flush to her body despite the blood she'd lost. When the violent bloodlust had faded in the aftermath of a crashing orgasm, they'd both been in shock. A moment later, the doors had opened, and... then what? What had happened next? No matter how hard she tried to remember, all that came was the memory of terrible vertigo followed by darkness.

She had no idea where Xander was right now, or even if he was alive or dead. A thread of fresh panic wove its way into her consciousness. Since she was here, it meant Crank must have either come for her himself, or sent his lackeys to retrieve her. Either way, it would have been painfully obvious to whoever opened the door what had happened inside that stuffy freezer. She still reeked of sex and blood even after having been hit with a bucket of water.

Crank must have *completely lost his mind* when he found out. He'd wanted to be the one to mate her, after all.

Would he kill Xander and try to take her for himself regardless? The thought made her gorge rise. Before, her wolf had been resigned to the idea of him taking her as a mate, even though the human part of her had been repulsed. Now, the very thought of it brought red, animal rage roaring in its wake.

She would not accept Crank as her mate. She was *already* mated. She knew that her wolf would fight any such attempt to the death, regardless of the fact that Crank was bigger, stronger, and more dominant than she was. None of those things mattered to the wolf anymore. The wolf had mated another, and that was that. But was her mate still alive?

Vampires are notoriously difficult to kill, Xander had said. Even so, he'd seemed as weakened as she was in the aftermath of their rage and lust-fueled coupling. He wasn't indestructible. Vampires could apparently still die. Kovac's guards had carried iron daggers for a reason when they'd kidnapped her and Sangye. And if folklore was to be believed, vampires had other vulnerabilities, as well. Wooden stakes. Sunlight. Decapitation.

If Crank was set on killing Xander, he could probably manage to do it.

Yet, some completely irrational corner of her mind insisted that if he were dead, she would know it somehow. She would feel an absence—an empty gap that was supposed to be filled by a stunningly attractive, sarcastic English son of a bitch with a voice that could make the phonebook sound seductive and long-fingered hands whose gentleness belied his cool, sardonic facade.

No. She would work on the assumption that Xander was still alive. Besides, whether he was or he wasn't, his friends were supposedly coming for Sangye soon. She just had to hang on until then.

She needed a plan. She needed to stall for time. A large part of her wanted to wear her defiance like a cloak for Crank and the whole world to see, but that would not help keep her alive and Sangye safe. As much as the idea made her want to retch, it would be better to play innocent and pretend to go along with whatever Crank wanted. She would just have to hope that Crank wouldn't immediately try to claim her physically. because she knew that neither she nor the wolf would submit to that without a fight.

"Sangye," she croaked, "Try not to be afraid. I need to rest for a bit, but they'll bring me in to see you shortly, I think."

She thought she heard him reply, but exhaustion and queasiness were already pulling her down.

-o-o-o-

Movement outside of her cell brought her back to awareness. She was still in the same position, lying naked on the bare floor with her shackled arms chained to a heavy metal ring on the wall. She blinked rapidly until her vision cleared and looked at the manacles properly for the first time. They were a very light colored, shiny metal, and the skin of her wrists was bright red and blistered beneath them. Even the smallest motion made the metal burn like fire against her flesh, and she caught her breath.

She stared at the shackles. Were they... silver? They had that sort of pale white cast beneath the metallic sheen that reminded her of silver jewelry, certainly. And it made a certain kind of sense. Werewolves. Silver bullets. Maybe there *was* a kernel of truth to the old superstitions.

She thought silver was supposed to be a soft metal, and considered trying to get free from them. But she had a suspicion that the pain from trying to do so would send her right back into a dead faint.

The cell door opened, and Tag came in. He kept his eyes averted from her body, and cleared his throat nervously.

"Hey," he said. "Uh, I'm supposed to give you this and see how you're doing."

He held up a chunk of meat, and Manisha's stomach cramped with sudden hunger, its earlier nausea forgotten in an instant. Tag handed it over to her cautiously as she stretched out to take it from him. She tore into it with her teeth, her wolf silently daring him to comment.

He didn't.

Instead, he said, "Look... Crank is with that creepy Eastern European guy right now. He'll be coming for you after they're done, though. I'm gonna bring you a bucket of water and a rag. It might help if you, um, clean yourself up a bit before he gets here. He's, uh... he's pretty pissed."

Manisha swallowed a mouthful of mutton and pinned Tag with her gaze. He glanced at her, flushed a bit, and looked down again. Her wolf snarled in triumph, confident in her dominance over him.

"What happened to the vampire?" she asked, trying her best to keep her voice cold and clipped.

"I dunno," Tag muttered. "Crank had Sawbones get iron shackles for him, and then they talked for a minute but I couldn't hear what they were saying. Sawbones disappeared for a bit and came back in time to ride here with us in the lorry, but he didn't say anything to me about the vamp."

She nodded to indicate she'd heard and went back to the meat, ignoring his presence. He shifted his feet for a few seconds.

"I'll, um, just go and get that bucket, I guess," he said after a brief, awkward silence, and left the cell, shutting the door after him.

Manisha finished the mutton, feeling a bit stronger once she had, even though she wanted to tear the blasted shackles off of her burning wrists. Tag returned with the bucket as promised, and put it within her reach before hastily retreating from the cell.

For the first time, she was truly starting to understand the power of the pack structure — as if transforming for the first time had merged her humanity and her wolf into a single being, allowing her to tap into that power and finally understand it rather than simply being a victim to it. No matter what Crank wanted to believe, she was a mated alpha werewolf female now — and Tag, at least, could sense that.

She licked the last of the grease and meat juices from her fingers, tasting traces of Xander's blood on them as she did so. That faint, metallic saltiness filled her senses and unleashed a new craving in her belly, despite the meal she'd just finished. Without really examining what she was doing, she licked at the rust-colored stain on the back of her hand, feeling the dried blood explode across her tongue in a vibrant bouquet.

She pulled back, shocked. What... on... earth?

Her wolf perked up, snuffling at the scent of blood, and relaxed again as if to say that blood was good—but that *fresh* blood would be better. She lifted her fingers to brush at the aching fang marks in the sensitive skin at the side of her neck, and shivered. She had no idea what her unexpected reaction to blood meant, and she also didn't know enough about the strange new world into which she'd been thrust to speculate.

For now, she focused on cleaning herself up as best she could, while firmly pushing down the bizarre and frankly alarming urge to suck the pinkish stains from the worn cloth of the old rag she was using to wash.

Her goal was to remove as much of the smell of sex and Xander from her body as she could before Crank got here. Without soap and a proper shower, she suspected that was going to be a losing fight—but it couldn't hurt. If she was going to play the innocent victim, the fewer reminders Crank had of what had happened in the freezer, the better.

TWELVE

Crank came for her less than an hour later. She still felt awful; she still smelled faintly of blood and... other bodily fluids. And there was still an unpleasant gnawing sensation in her belly despite the meat she'd eaten. Her wolf still wanted to tear something's head off. All in all, this conversation was probably not going to go as smoothly as one might hope.

The alpha glared at her as the door slammed behind him. It took her a fraction longer than it should have to remember that she was supposed to look down submissively. Apparently, her wolf's attitude toward the pack leader had changed. She just hoped she could play the part of innocent victim well enough to fool him without relying on the wolf's social cues for guidance in how to act.

A tatty robe or wrap of some kind hit her in the chest and fell to the grimy floor.

"Put that on," Crank growled.

How am I supposed to get dressed when my wrists are chained to the wall, you half-wit? she thought irritably. But she swallowed down every last trace of her contempt before saying, "Could you please take my shackles off so I can do that, Crank?"

Crank grumbled something, but pulled a key out of his pocket and released the silver manacles one at a time. "If you try to run again, Manisha, things are going to get ugly. And it won't be your hide taking the lashing. It'll be the boy's."

Manisha kept her eyes down and nodded as though his words had cowed her. She pulled on the threadbare cover-up before she spoke.

"I won't run again. I'm sorry, Crank. I was scared, and I thought since Sangye was a vampire that maybe another vampire would help him. I won't make that mistake again. The bastard raped me while I was still disoriented from the transformation. I tried to fight him off, but he was so strong—"

Her wolf bristled at the fabrication, growling, and Manisha was right there with the animal, really. What kind of a person did it make her to be able to spout glib lies about such a thing? Of course, what kind of person did it make her that in reality, she'd been the one to assault *him*?

Mate, the wolf thought possessively. *Mine*.

No. She had to concentrate on survival now, for both her and Sangye. No matter how messed up this whole situation had become, the important thing was to hold on and stay alive. If she had to act like a lying, conniving, manipulative bitch to do that… well, so be it. She wasn't doing it just to save herself. She was doing it to save Sangye.

Crank's meaty hand tipped her chin up, and the touch made her skin crawl. Holding in the shudder that wanted to shake free, she glanced up at his angry gaze for only an instant before letting her eyes slide down and to the side again.

"Vampires are evil," Crank said in a hard tone. "That's why Kovac is trying to capture them—so he can put them down like the rabid animals they are. Sawbones shouldn't've trapped one of them in there with you. But you also shouldn't have let the filthy creature live. You should've killed him."

"I tried, Crank," she said, trying to inject as much pathos into the words as possible. "He was too strong."

He let her chin go abruptly, like he was suddenly disgusted with her. "I can't believe you let a vampire touch you like that. Jesus." He huffed out a disgruntled breath. "Kovac wants you to make the boy feed—no more pussyfooting around with it. But tonight, maybe I'll show you how a real man fucks a woman. Wipe those vampire handprints right off of your skin until you don't even remember what he did to you."

Nausea roiled in Manisha's aching gut as the wolf lunged inside her, battering at her mind and demanding she try to rip out this presumptuous male's throat. Tears burned against the backs of her eyes at the certain knowledge that if she couldn't get out of this mess by tonight, she was as good as dead. She would not submit to Crank, and he was too strong for her to win the fight. It was all she could do to nod agreeably, not looking up from the floor.

A large hand yanked her to unsteady feet. "C'mon. Kovac wants the brat to feed right away. No excuses."

As they entered the other cell, Manisha's chest ached upon seeing how frail and gaunt Sangye looked.

"Kumari?" he asked weakly. "Are you well?"

"I'm fine," she told him, knowing that she sounded very far from *fine*. "Sangye, please. You must feed today. You're growing very weak. Please... do it for me."

As if her words had been a signal, Bastian Kovac dragged a skinny teenage boy into the cell by the back of his neck. The boy's eyes seemed glazed and distant. He didn't speak or cry out when Kovac hurled him down at Sangye's feet. Almost immediately, the enclosed space filled with a reeking cloud of cologne and rot. It was all Manisha could do not to gag.

"Just..." She swallowed hard. "Just take a little. *Please*. Not enough to hurt him. Just enough to give you strength. Sangye, I'm scared for you."

Sangye closed his eyes. He looked dizzy, as though he were having trouble focusing. "I am sorry, Kumari Sadhu. I cannot do as you ask." His eyes fluttered open, an unnatural glow emanating from their depths.

Manisha wasn't feeling too steady on her own feet, so she was unable to scramble away when Kovac strode over and dragged her backward, wrapping one thick-muscled arm around her neck. She gasped, then gagged at his stench pressed so close to her. Sangye's eyes glowed brighter, a look of anguish sliding over his hollow-cheeked face.

"I will make this very simple for you, whelp," said Kovac. "Drink the human's blood, or I will snap your nursemaid's neck and rip her head from her body. I assure you, that method of execution is highly effective on all creatures... even werewolves."

Manisha's breath was locked in her ribcage, leaving her powerless to say a word in either exhortation or denial. By contrast, Sangye's thin chest rose and fell like a bellows under the force of his emotions. She remembered Xander had said vampires didn't need to breathe, and hoped that hyperventilating like this wouldn't somehow hurt him. Kovac wrenched her head to the side, making her gasp in pain.

"I..." Sangye said faintly. "I... I can't..."

With that, his eyes rolled up in his head and he slumped bonelessly, held up only by the shackles around his wrists and throat.

Unconscious.

Manisha cried out and tried to lunge toward him despite Kovac's punishing grip. After a moment, Kovac made a noise of disgust and shoved her away. She stumbled to her knees near the teenager he had brought for Sangye to feed on. Staggering upright, she attempted to support Sangye in his chains, her stomach turning at the hissing sound as the iron bit into his flesh.

Crank dragged her away, and it was all Manisha could do not to turn on him then and there. But that would be suicide, she knew, and if she were dead, Sangye would be left all alone at the mercy of these evil men.

-o-o-o-

Bastian Kovac tilted his head to one side and scrutinized the unconscious vampire child through the dark lenses of his sunglasses.

"Disappointing," he observed philosophically. Unfortunately, the failure to get the whelp feeding was merely one among a number of things that were currently disappointing him. Perhaps it was finally time to do something about that situation.

"We can try again when he comes around," Crank muttered.

Yes, Kovac decided, *it was definitely time.*

He'd known when he'd first enlisted the help of London's werewolves that he would be surrounding himself with rampant stupidity, but the pack's leader had turned out to be even more of a simpleton than Kovac had originally expected. While the beast had managed to find and lure another of the vampires to this abandoned warehouse, that act was really the only thing he hadn't failed at doing.

There had been little question that the nightcrawler would be able to escape the werewolves after confirming the presence of the vampire child. That fact suited Kovac and his Master well enough, since it allowed him to contact his fellow bloodsuckers and draw the prey Kovac truly wanted into the net.

He needed the vampire called Snag.

With the woman Manisha now turned into a werewolf, she was safely out of her potential vampire mate's grasp. That meant neither of them posed any real threat to his Master at this point. Even with the temporary addition of the boy Sangye to the vampires' ranks, the prophesied Council of Thirteen was broken before it could ever form.

Now, it was almost time to win the war. Because the Mighty and Most High Bael was not at war with the vampires. He never had been. No, He was at war with the Angel Israfael. And to bring the Angel out of hiding so He could defeat her, He would need the oldest and most powerful of His failures—the vampire Snag.

The alpha werewolf was a fool. He'd held his rival—his sworn enemy—within his grip, weakened and helpless. And rather than kill the injured vampire, Crank had concocted a ridiculous plan for torture and revenge, ordering the nightcrawler chained in iron and left to burn in the sun.

Kovac had briefly considered forbidding the foolhardy endeavor and driving a stake through the creature's heart then and there. However, he'd sensed that the other vampires had arrived in the city, and changed his mind. The search for their endangered comrade would draw them into the open. If they managed to save him, he would lead them all right back here, into Bael's trap.

And if they didn't manage to save him? Well, it was reasonably likely the captured vampire had already given them the location of the warehouse, and they would still come. However, they would enter the battle distracted and upset after the tragic loss of one of their own. So, Kovac had allowed Crank his folly, quietly using his mental influence to ensure that the werewolf left behind as a guard and witness to the vampire's death wandered off as soon as the rest of them had gone.

Outside, the sun was going down. It was time to move the chess pieces into position.

"Take the woman back to her cell and shackle her again," he ordered.

"I want some time alone with her first," the alpha growled. "She and I have business."

Kovac saw the woman cringe at Crank's words, but he ignored it. "Later," he said carelessly.

Crank bristled, though he submitted under Kovac's flat stare, as Kovac had known he would. Grumbling, the alpha dragged the woman away from the vampire whelp, shaking her a bit when she tried to protest. The boy continued to hang limp in his shackles, oblivious to the burn of iron against his pale skin. Kovac turned his back on the child and followed Crank into the other cell, ensuring that the woman was secured in the silver shackles as he had directed.

"Leave the door open," he told Crank when the werewolf started to swing the heavy wood shut. "I want her to see this."

If the vampires were close enough to hear it, her screams of horror might draw them — especially if the one who'd once been her mate was still alive.

Crank's face furrowed in confusion. "What do you want her to see?" he asked stupidly.

"My Master's power," Kovac said, and closed his eyes.

He reached out, mentally prostrating himself before the might of Bael. Supplicating Him for the honor of His dark presence. The tiny hairs on Kovac's arms stood up as electricity crackled around the dingy basement, and Crank took an involuntary step back, looking around nervously.

"What the hell?" the werewolf asked, his fists clenching as though he could defend against the oncoming Darkness by punching it.

Kovac laughed, the sound growing high-pitched and unhinged as black, oily fog rolled into the warehouse through tiny cracks in the walls and floor.

"What is that?" the woman chained in silver cried from inside her cell. "What's happening—what are you doing?"

The dark mist billowed up around the were-wolves, who choked and scrabbled at their own skin, trying to free themselves from the grip of the Darkness.

"What am I doing, whore?" Kovac asked, the words emerging almost gleeful. "Why, I am merely baiting the trap, preparing it in time for the prey to arrive."

THIRTEEN

When Xander next woke, Snag was crouched in the shadows a few feet away from him, sitting on his heels with his arms resting loosely across his knees. The old scarecrow's head was tilted to one side as he regarded Xander with a vaguely quizzical expression. Xander squeezed his eyes shut and blinked rapidly, trying to rid himself of the feeling that someone had glued emery powder to the insides of his eyelids.

The sun had made its passage across the open sky above while he'd lain insensible, and was now about to disappear behind the buildings on the opposite side of the road. Xander looked down at his bare torso, taking in unhealed wounds. His skin was flushed faintly pink with the sort of sunburn that afflicted careless humans at the beach, rather than the sort that turned vampires into charred meat.

Snag's deep, arresting mental voice interrupted his musings. *Little brother*, he asked conversationally, *what in the gods' names have you done?*

His tone carried the same sense of gentle chiding as a parent whose toddler had just jumped in a mud puddle, and Xander tried not to chafe under it.

"Snag—a little help here, mate?" he rasped. "If you wouldn't mind?"

Snag looked significantly at him, and then at the western sky, where the sun had not quite disappeared behind the roofline.

"Oh," Xander said, deflating. "Right."

Snag had never been what one might call a brilliant conversationalist, so Xander was a bit surprised when another question followed.

What attacked you? Your wounds are not healing properly.

Xander snorted and let his head fall back against the steel of the bike rack. With difficulty, he resisted the urge to smack his skull against it a couple more times for good measure.

"Ah-*woooo*!" he rasped, laying on as much irony as he could muster. "Werewolves of London..."

Silence greeted the quip.

"Never mind," he sighed. "Wrong audience. Damn it, I'd been saving that one for just the right moment, too." More of the past couple of days started to filter back into his consciousness, and he sobered. "Shit. *Shit*. Are the others here?"

He started shuffling around to the position he'd started in, which was now mostly in shadow. He felt Snag push awareness of his links with the others into his mind. Eris and Trynn, relatively nearby. Della and Tré, quite a distance away. Of course. They hadn't known where to find him once his captors had taken him away from the butcher's shop, so they'd split up.

Snag sent out a powerful, wordless call along the bond, and Xander nearly passed out again.

"*Nngh*," he groaned, trying very hard not to lose his stomach contents for the first time in more than a hundred twenty years. "Was that *really* necessary? Still feeling a bit delicate over here."

When he peeled open his eyelids again, Snag was at his side—the side with the shadows, obviously. One wiry arm extended within reach of Xander's fangs.

"I'm not sure blood loss is the problem, old chap," he rasped. "Something else is wrong with me, I think."

True, he'd lost blood, but not vast amounts, as evidenced by the fact that some of his wounds were still bleeding. Snag gave a mental shrug, as if to say, *do you have any better ideas*? Which, of course, Xander didn't, so he huffed a breath and bit into the pale skin he was offered.

Oddly enough, this was the first time he'd ever fed from Snag directly. And to be honest, up until recently he would have felt rather guilty in doing so, since the old ghoul never looked as though he had enough blood for himself, much less someone else. In the past few weeks, though, Snag had surprised them all by agreeing to feed from both Eris and Trynn. The difference that regular feeding had wrought in him was startling—his body, though still strikingly lean, was no longer skeletal, and his skin no longer resembled crackling parchment. A smattering of dark hair had even started to sprout on his eyebrows.

As Xander swallowed the first mouthful of that ancient blood, he took a moment to be grateful that Snag had been the one to find him. The old sod had been frighteningly powerful even when he seemed perpetually on the verge of becoming a petrified mummy. Now, his blood offered a kick like rocket fuel.

Xander's stomach wasn't too pleased about much of anything at that point, but the rest of him sure as hell appreciated the boost. His vision cleared and the world stopped spinning like a carnival ride. His skin itched as his flesh knitted back together. The trembling weakness in his limbs subsided.

There is a new kind of darkness residing within you, Snag observed as he pulled away.

Xander ignored the words and awkwardly wiped one manacled hand across his mouth. "Later. Bastian Kovac is here," he said, sounding more like himself. "He's got my mate. Which means that right now, we've got undead arse to kick." He took a breath and focused inward. "I still can't shift form. In the absence of the key to these shackles, I think we'll need to do this the old-fashioned way."

Snag's expression had hardened at the mention of Kovac's name. His gnarled fingers closed around the length of iron chain attached to Xander's wrist shackles. Xander winced at the sound of hissing and crackling as the iron burned Snag's skin, only to realize an instant later that it was not doing the same to him. In fact... it hadn't been burning him since he regained consciousness.

He put that tidbit away to ponder later, along with the part where he'd spent a few hours in direct sunlight with no real harm to show for it. Right now, there were more important things to worry about.

Coordinating mentally with Snag, he wrenched backward with all his might, his strength bolstered by the older vampire's. The iron chain snapped at its weakest link. They repeated the process with the chain shackling his legs, and finally his neck. Xander staggered to his feet without grace. He gathered up the lengths of hanging chain that were long enough to drag on the ground if he didn't, cursing both them and his inability to shift.

"Right. Where are we?" he snapped.

Snag sent him a mental snapshot of their location relative to the river, and he took a moment to orient himself against the mental map he had of his home city. Not far from Battersea, it appeared — thank god.

"The others can catch up with us on the way," he said, and took off at a run, heading for the first intersection where he could go west. Snag swirled into mist, pacing him. Xander cursed under his breath at the way the heavy shackles hampered his gait. If his sudden inability to shift was permanent, it was going to end up being a serious bitch.

They'd gone nearly four blocks through the deserted factory district before Xander heard the rumble of an elderly Vauxhall Astra in need of a tune-up heading in their direction. He stopped the car by the simple expedient of stepping into the roadway in front of it and raising one manacled hand, palm out.

Brakes squealed. Xander met the startled driver's eyes through the windscreen. Thankfully, he hadn't lost the ability to mentally influence humans, and thirty seconds later he was settling into the back seat. Snag materialized silently next to him as the Astra peeled out and did a U-turn, heading for Battersea as fast as the aging one-point-four-liter diesel would take them.

The journey could not have been more than two miles, but it seemed to take forever in the deepening dusk. A dark, winged shape swooped low enough to be visible through the window, and was joined a moment later by a second one, smaller and lighter-colored.

Xander? Eris' mental voice questioned.

Where are the others? Xander shot back, unwilling to take time for pleasantries.

Hello to you, too, came Trynn's dry voice. *Tré and Della started searching closer to your apartment and business headquarters. Nice digs, by the way. What does your company do? I never thought to ask before. Whatever it is, it's apparently pretty lucrative.*

Ask me when I'm not focused on the best way to turn a certain undead Slavic bastard into pulverized road kill, Xander growled.

Trynn immediately sobered. *You'll have to join the queue. Do we know what the hell Kovac's even doing here?*

Not a goddamned clue, beyond the obvious — trying to fuck our lives over more thoroughly than they've already been fucked. He clenched his jaw, remembering that there hadn't been a chance to pass on one very important piece of information to the others. *There's something you all need to know. This boy, he's not just some random kid.*

He took a breath.

Go on, Eris prompted.

Xander shook his head in frustration. *Sangye Rinchen was on his way to meet with the Tibetan Lama Regent when his motorcade was attacked in India.*

Snag's head whipped around, his dark eyes burning holes through Xander far more effectively than the sun had managed to do earlier.

The Lama Regent? Eris echoed. *You don't mean…*

Xander closed his eyes. *Yeah — I do mean. Manisha says Sangye is considered a candidate to be the fifteenth Dalai Lama.*

Complete silence fell across the link, broken only by the rough purr of the car's engine and the occasional honk of a horn as the mesmerized driver cut through traffic.

Then, Eris let out a string of mixed Latin and Cypriot Greek curses, creative and filthy enough that Xander was momentarily impressed despite the dire circumstances.

Do you realize what this means? Eris demanded, still sounding like he wanted to tear someone's head off.

I realize plenty, Xander snapped across the bond. *But right now, the only thing I give a tinker's damn about is the fact that Manisha has been in Kovac's hands for the better part of a day. I'm sure I don't have to remind everyone here what he managed to do to* you *during that length of time.*

That might have been a low blow, but it effectively drove home the point he was trying to make.

He could feel Trynn's simmering anger at the memory of what had happened to Eris after his ill-conceived reconnaissance mission into Kovac's territory outside of Damascus.

The others should be here soon, was all she said, as the Astra careened around a corner, ignoring a red light.

I'm not waiting. Xander would have crossed his arms stubbornly at that point, but the iron manacles made that impossible. Once again, he tried to reach into his center and transform his body into vapor. It had exactly the same effect as before — which was to say, none at all.

Wait. I felt that, Eris said with the mental equivalent of a frown. *Something else is wrong. What the hell happened to you?*

Snag raised a slow eyebrow at Xander as if to say, *this I have to hear.* Xander scowled at him. But… they were going to learn the details sooner or later, assuming they didn't all end up dead before dawn. And the information might end up being important, even though it was also embarrassing as fuck.

"I might or might not've been sexually assaulted by a half-turned werewolf in a way that also involved a fair amount of mutual biting and… uh… blood exchange," he muttered aloud, knowing the others would be able to pick it up through the bond.

Aaand… there was that dead silence again, exacerbated this time by the extremely odd expression Snag suddenly seemed to be wearing.

You bit a werewolf? Eris asked eventually, sounding almost insulted. *I thought you hated werewolves.*

"She bit me first!" he burst out, and then took a centering breath. *Look – she was out of control, and I thought draining her might calm her down.*

Uh-huh, Trynn drawled. *I bet that's what you tell all the girls.*

Shut up, Trynn. It… well. It sort of worked, he threw back sullenly. *Only now, I can't shift form, and I feel like two-day-old shit even after a double-shot of Snag's super espresso blood.*

Snag shot him another dark look.

Oh, Xander added. *And I, uh, spent several hours in direct sunlight with only a bit of a tan to show for it. Also, iron doesn't burn me anymore.*

Another beat of silence before Eris' rather shell-shocked response. *You… what, now?*

Xander was vaguely aware of Eris directing a question privately to Snag, probably double-checking his story, and of the older vampire's mental shrug of confirmation.

Whoa, Trynn said. *So, you can go out in daylight now? Seriously? Do you think it's permanent, or just some weird temporary thing?*

His teeth ground together. *How the hell should I know?*

Enough. We are close. Snag's commanding mental voice cut through the link.

Peering out the window, Xander confirmed that Snag was right. He wondered if that meant his companion could sense Sangye directly.

Yes, Snag confirmed. *I can.*

-o-o-o-

Manisha watched in terror through the open door of her cell as black mist swirled around the basement, choking the figures of the other werewolves. They cried out and writhed, clutching at their throats.

"No!" she shouted, ignoring the burning pain of the silver against her skin as she jerked against her chains. "Stop! *You're killing them!*"

She could just make out a low moan coming from Sangye in the cell next to hers. He was regaining consciousness. She struggled harder to get free, but the agonizing shock of the silver against her flesh threatened to send her to her knees. She subsided, panting.

"Kumari Sadhu!" Sangye called weakly. "What is it, what's happening?"

Just then, Crank appeared in the door of her cell, oily black fog coiled around his neck and body like tentacles.

"This is your fault! *Your fault!*" he roared, stumbling toward her. "*Why couldn't you just kill the fucker like you were supposed to!*"

He fell to the ground inches away from her, and a cry lodged in her throat as he scrabbled at the strangling fog, the light gradually fading from his accusing eyes until his arms flopped to the ground and lay limp.

This isn't because of me, she thought desperately, staring down at Crank's dead form. *It isn't me — it's the dark fog! Kovac's ancient evil! It isn't my fault!*

A tendril of the darkness unfurled, brushing her naked leg in a caress that burned as painfully as the silver. She clenched her eyes shut, suppressed tears making her chest jerk, and waited to die.

"Kumari Sadhu!" Sangye cried again, more fear in his voice this time. "*Kumari Sadhu!*"

"I'm sorry, Sangye," she whispered. "I tried. I tried to save us…"

Cool fingers grabbed her chin, reeking of cologne and decay. Her eyes flew open.

"Yes, so you did. That will probably be your last mistake," Bastian Kovac said in a low, intimate tone. "Never fear, though. My Master has one remaining use for you." He kicked Crank's corpse onto its side with one patent leather-clad foot. "Your pack leader was a fool. But you will still make highly effective bait for one vampire in particular… assuming his fellow nightcrawlers arrived in time to rescue him from the sun's rays."

Hatred leant Manisha a degree of courage she wouldn't otherwise have had, and she spit at Kovac's face, glaring into the reflective lenses of his dark glasses. The gob missed, hitting his shirt collar instead. He only let out a contemptuous huff of air through his nose, and released her chin with a disdainful little shove.

"Just like all the other vampires' whores," he said with a scornful sneer. "If your worthless cur of a lover does decide to show up, I'll make sure to let you watch as he dies in agony."

"Fuck you," Manisha whispered, her heart pounding against her chest as though trying to escape the cage of her ribs.

Kovac whipped out a perfectly folded pocket-handkerchief and wiped the gob of spit from his collar before tossing it at her feet. "I wouldn't stoop to dirty myself with your rotten hole, slut." He turned to the door, and the bodies littering the warehouse floor beyond. "Now, watch and learn."

He stretched out his arms, the tendons in his hands and fingers standing out as though he were lifting some invisible weight. His head fell back, lips curling into a rictus as power thrummed around the enclosed space.

"No…" Sangye moaned in the next cell, barely audible. "No, no, no…"

At Manisha's feet, Crank's corpse twitched and stirred. She gasped, trying to scramble backward even though she was already pressed against the wall. His eyes snapped open, lifeless and filmy. Limbs moving in a grotesque parody of life, the alpha werewolf rose to his feet and wavered for a moment, catching himself with a hand pressed to the wall on either side of her body. His huge frame towered over her; his dead eyes stared right through her. As she watched, aghast, a tiny droplet of drool trailed from the corner of his slack mouth.

Finally pushed beyond her limits, Manisha threw back her head and shrieked, again and again and again.

-o-o-o-

Xander met their unwitting chauffeur's glazed eyes in the rearview mirror. "Stop here," he told the man, unwilling to drag an innocent human any further into this mess. "Let us out, resume obeying the traffic laws, and drive back to where you found us. Then forget you ever saw us or stopped for us."

The Astra screeched to a halt. Xander was out of the vehicle an instant later, Snag swirling around him in a vaporous cloud as he, too, exited. Xander slammed the door behind him, and the car drove off sedately. A flurry of broad wings stirred the air on either side of him as Trynn and Eris dropped lightly to the ground in human form.

Eris raked his eyes up and down Xander's body once, and Xander could well imagine what he was seeing. No shirt, pink scars littering his body — still not completely faded even after drinking from Snag. Iron clamped around his wrists, ankles, and neck. Trousers held up by a single button that was hanging on by a thread — the ripped zipper having succumbed without protest to Manisha's assault in the freezer.

To his credit, all Eris said was, "Do you want me to see if I can pick the locks on those shackles? Trynn, have you got a hairpin or something?"

"Fuck the shackles," Xander said. "Come on."

"Wait," Eris said. "Weapons. We raided your flat."

"Guns won't be much use," he pointed out, impatient to be moving.

Trynn scowled at him, and pulled out a couple of daggers. "Give us a bit of credit, yeah? Were-wolves. Silver. Even I've heard of that one. Though, do I really want to know why you keep a small arsenal of silver-bladed knives in your spare bedroom?"

He accepted the two sheathed daggers from her and a belt with half a dozen smaller throwing blades from Eris... which had the added benefit of reducing the likelihood that his battered trousers would end up around his ankles during a fight.

"London is one of the few major cities in the world with a standing werewolf population," he told Trynn.

"Just like in the song, huh?" she said.

His lips thinned. "Too late. I already used that one. Now, *come on.*"

They jogged quickly toward the warehouse. At least, he, Trynn, and Eris jogged, making Xander wish almost immediately that he'd let Eris take a stab at unlocking the damned shackles after all. Snag had vanished into mist again, not being a big one for traveling on foot.

They'd covered about half of the remaining distance when a piercing female scream of rage and horror nearly split Xander's skull in two. He staggered and nearly fell, catching himself on a hand and a knee, his other hand flying to clutch at his temple. A strong grip pulled him upright, but he shook it off, stumbling back a step.

"Manisha," he whispered.

"Xander," Eris said, "what is it? Are you in mental contact with her?"

Before he could formulate an answer, the scream came again, a noise containing all the terrified denial of someone witnessing a nightmare brought to life. Blood-hot rage welled up inside Xander like a volcanic eruption, demanding to be unleashed on whoever was responsible for making his mate sound like that. His limbs twisted as if his body could not contain the incandescent torrent of anger in its human form, and needed to become something else to accommodate it.

This was not the familiar morphing into winged flight or swirling vapor, however. It was something new. More powerful. More dangerous. He fell to all fours, the shackles falling from his wrists and ankles with a clatter. He was only vaguely aware of Eris snarling, "What the *hell*?" as he pressed Trynn protectively behind his body.

Xander threw back his head, and howled.

Fourteen

The wolf scrambled free of the shackles that had bound Xander's wrists and ankles in human form, his slender legs slipping out easily now. With a hard shake, he dislodged the heavy iron ring that hung around his neck. He fought his way loose from the torn remains of his trousers, the belt with the knives following them down to the ground.

The movement made him stagger sideways when his body didn't respond the way he was expecting, but he steadied himself stiffly on four splayed legs a moment later. His memory flashed back to Manisha struggling to gain control of her wolf form, and he knew he didn't have time for that. She had been panicked, and in physical agony. It was also the first experience she'd ever had with physical transformation.

Xander had been able to alter his form into something complete different for more than a century, and while he was fighting panic for Manisha after hearing her mental cry, becoming a wolf did not frighten him. Hell, anything that got him out of the manacles and lent him added running speed was peachy *fucking* keen with him right now.

Xander? Eris was still shielding Trynn behind him, though she was hopping up and down impatiently, trying to get a better look at him.

"What the hell just happened?" she asked. "Is that him?"

Snag had also graced them with his solid presence once more, staring at Xander warily from a few paces away.

Xander growled at them both mentally and aloud, needing a moment's quiet to get his new legs sorted out. Eris stiffened, and he realized that might not have been the most reassuring response to their expressions of shock.

Just give me a damned minute, will you? he sent instead. *I've never been a fucking quadruped before.*

Eris and Snag relaxed their wary stances, and Trynn wriggled free from Eris' protective hold to dart forward and retrieve the knife belt, strapping it around her waist since it was going to be fairly useless to Xander now.

"So... is this what happens when a werewolf bites a vampire?" she asked. "Because... well... *damn.*"

Xander was only vaguely aware of the rather pointed look that passed between Eris and Snag, since he was more focused on mastering basic locomotion.

"I'm not aware that anyone has been stupid enough to test the hypothesis before," Eris said. "But under the circumstances, I'm going to go with *yes.*"

Something prickled along Xander's awareness, and a moment later, two new presences materialized next to the others.

"What... on... *earth*...?" Della said faintly.

Tré blinked twice—for him, an expression of profound shock. Xander narrowed his eyes.

"Do I want to know?" Tré asked.

No, he sent.

"No," Eris confirmed.

"Yes," Trynn countered, "but not now. Xander, can you run?"

Xander trotted a few strides in the direction they needed to go. Rangy muscles propelled his long legs over the ground without effort, the rhythm quickly becoming natural. After a few moments he accelerated into a lope, and then a full run, aware of the others keeping pace with him in the air, borne aloft on silent, powerful wings.

Hurry, he urged. *Hurry!*

-o-o-o-

Manisha trembled in reaction as the cell door closed and locked with a solid click behind Kovac and the… *thing* that had been Crank. The black fog had receded, leaving the cell empty but for her. Tears squeezed from between her tightly closed eyelids, burning her cheeks as they slid down. Outside, she heard rustling and shuffling sounds as the others underwent the same gruesome transformation.

Tag.

Patch.

Gillian.

Penny.

Lilith.

Sawbones, and all the rest.

The entire pack—those who had treated her decently, those who had treated her poorly, and those who had more or less ignored her. All dead now. Worse than dead.

Manisha had heard the news reports coming out of Syria. BBC reporters calmly describing corpses crawling from the rubble; trying to make the appearance of rampaging undead berserkers sound like some kind of radiation sickness after the bomb had gone off in Damascus, rather than what it truly was. Her mind had rejected what she'd seen and heard at the time, when it was just some distant story on the television.

Now, it was right in front of her.

"Why do this?" Sangye asked, his pained voice coming from the other side of the wall separating them. "*Why?*"

She didn't dare try to answer him, certain that all she'd be able to get out would be angry, terrified sobbing rather than any kind of comfort or reassurance. She had an awful feeling she knew the answer to why Kovac had perpetrated this new crime against nature.

The vampires were coming. And if this truly were like what was happening in Damascus, they would be met by a pack of opponents who couldn't be stopped by gunfire or any other normal means of fighting. But these weren't normal humans to begin with. These were werewolves. Could they be stopped at all?

-o-o-o-

The area around the warehouse seemed strangely deserted when Xander and the other vampires approached. There was no sign of any werewolves guarding the area or keeping watch over the entrance points. Xander barely slowed as he bypassed the door where he'd been escorted into the building, what seemed like years ago — though in reality it had only been days. He raced around the perimeter until he came to a broken window boasting a large enough gap for his lupine body to fit through without getting sliced to pieces, and leapt. Broken glass cut into his tough paw pads as he landed on the other side, but he ignored the sting.

The others swirled through in vaporous form and followed his lead.

What kind of resistance are we looking at here? Tré asked.

Two-dozen werewolves, max, he growled. *Not all of them fighters.*

Kovac is inside, Eris said grimly.

Leave him to Snag, Tré insisted in an uncompromising tone. *That's an order.*

It was an order that Xander had no intention of following if he managed to get his fangs anywhere near Kovac's throat. He also suspected he'd be fighting off Trynn for the privilege of drawing first blood, but he said nothing.

Somewhat surprisingly, it was Snag who spoke next. *Undead nearby,* he warned.

Xander didn't slow, but he did cast his senses outward.

Shit. Snag was right, and Xander didn't know how the presence of Bael's mindless foot soldiers tied in to what was happening here. Still…

It's not the first time we've faced them, he pointed out, *and it won't be the last.*

His comrades materialized around him, flanking him with silver blades drawn. He led the way unerringly for the stairwell leading to the basement — the dark, claustrophobic space where Manisha's hand had brushed his as she slipped a crumpled note into his pocket, upending his life and crumbling the ground from underneath his feet.

I'm coming, Manisha, he thought, projecting as strongly as he could. *We're coming for you. Hold on.*

-o-o-o-

We're coming for you. Hold on.

The words echoed in Manisha's mind, making her breath catch. Were they a hallucination? Wishful thinking? Or did she dare believe that Xander was still alive? That he and the other vampires were here?

And if they were here, did they have any idea of what they were about to encounter?

If it wasn't a hallucination, she wondered if Xander would be able to hear her in his mind the way she'd just heard him. But she was too horrified to concentrate on clearing or projecting her thoughts right now, and had no real idea how to approach such a thing anyway. Instead, she strained her ears, hoping for some hint of what was happening outside.

The cell door next to hers opened and closed. *Sangye.* Her heart pounded as she heard Kovac's deep, rough laugh.

"It is almost time for you to perform your first service for my Master, whelp," he said, low and threatening.

"I will not serve your Master," Sangye replied in a quavering voice. "I will not serve you."

Manisha held her breath. More laughter. The rattle of chains.

"Oh, I think you will," Kovac said. "But for the moment, we do not require your cooperation, boy. Only your existence."

Sangye cried out in surprise—a sound like a startled bird.

"Sangye!" Manisha called. She lunged against the silver manacles holding her to the wall, and gasped at the pain as they bit into her sore wrists. "*Sangye!*"

"Yes, by all means, keep crying out in fear, whore," Kovac said, sounding amused. "Help draw your nightcrawler and his friends into the trap for me."

She snapped her jaw shut, fear and rage washing through her veins in equal measure. Beyond the cells, the sound of running feet echoed through the warehouse, followed by the snarl of a maddened wolf. That snarl wove through her chest, tugging at something inside—calling like to like. Though she could not have explained how she knew it, her wolf recognized the sound of its mate and returned a silent, answering howl.

The animal battered at her mind, trying to get free. Manisha reeled under the assault and dropped to her knees. Her eyes fell on the silver rings binding her wrists. She caught her breath, looking at them—realization hitting her all at once. The other werewolves had said nothing about the possibility of shifting form outside of the night of the full moon, but she could feel that the wolf inside her cared nothing for any of that.

Her wolf… wanted *out*.

As the sounds of battle erupted outside, Manisha narrowed her eyes at the silver shackles and let the animal take control. The wrenching transformation overtook her, less painful than it had been under the pull of the moon. Her body twisted, arms and hands changing into slender legs and paws that slipped free of the burning metal restraints, leaving her free.

The she-wolf shook her furry head, gaining balance and control quickly this time. Outside, her mate battled the undead specters of her former pack. She needed to be with him, fighting at his side, but the heavy door still stood between them. As she had done in the abandoned freezer, Manisha lunged at it, snarling in frustration and battering her body against the heavy wood.

-o-o-o-

Snag glided noiselessly into the shadowy basement, his senses spreading outward, unsurprised by what he found. Undead werewolves stood arrayed in the area beyond the stairwell's landing—a nightmare of his own making, now raised to a new level of horror by the power of Bael's darkness.

He felt realization sweep through his comrades; felt them hesitate... all except for Xander. The youngest and brashest of the Originals cared only for the fact that the lifeless figures stood between him and his mate. Which was as it should be—as long as that brashness didn't result in his death during a moment of distraction.

There were three presences in the warehouse who required Snag's immediate attention. The first was a wolf who still lived, and who shared the same strange tangle of powers that Xander now exhibited. He could hear her battering at the door of her prison, heedless of the damage to herself in the face of her need to join her mate.

An uncertain future awaited Snag behind the second locked door, but before he faced that future, he would at least do this for his friends. In front of him, Xander's powerful wolf-form slammed into the nearest puppet soldier, teeth and claws ripping. The others followed an instant later, outnumbered but determined.

Snag ignored the battle, effortlessly shifting into mist and slipping past the figures locked in mortal combat. Silver and iron blades flashed in the dim light. The warehouse was eerily silent except for Xander's growling and the answering howls emerging from behind the first door.

He rematerialized in front of the cell and examined the locking mechanism, ignoring the sounds of animal rage coming from within. The door itself was wood, but heavy and well seasoned.

Even so, it was no match for a millennia-old vampire's focused strength.

He grasped the handle and set his feet, reaching inside himself. With a violent burst of controlled motion, he wrenched the door outward, splintering the wood around the metal bolt. It swung open on creaking hinges, disgorging a bristling blur of gray and white. Xander's mate headed straight for the undead werewolf he was battling and slammed into the creature's legs, downing it beneath a flurry of tearing fangs.

Snag had seen Xander's sense of the woman Manisha in his thoughts and memories—a gentle, loving person raised in a non-violent religion and possessed of a giving spirit. He hoped she would allow herself leniency for such violence against beings whose souls had already fled, leaving behind only empty shells. The path she now faced was difficult enough without the sort of guilt that he and the five other original vampires wore around their necks like millstones.

One of the werewolf husks stumbled toward him, its arms outstretched. Snag bared his fangs at it. The creature was too new for the stench of rot to have grown overpowering, but the reek of spiritual emptiness was just as grating to his acute senses. It reached for his throat and he thrust power outward, knocking it back a step.

There was only one thing to be done for such a creature in the absence of silver. Snag pounced, grabbing its skull in both hands and twisting with the same explosive strength he'd used to snap the lock on the door. There was a crack of bone... a wet, tearing sound... and the undead werewolf's head hit the concrete floor with a dull *thud* before rolling a short distance away. The body staggered forward a step, and Snag moved neatly out of its path. The arms jerked and waved as if for balance, then the large frame fell to its knees and toppled over. Its fingers continued to twitch as if attempting to drag itself toward him.

He ignored it in favor of doing a quick scan of the others, all of whom were still alive and fighting. *Beheading is effective*, he sent, noting that Xander and his werewolf mate had also had success with tearing off limbs until the torso could no longer locomote efficiently. Confident that they would look after each other and eventually prevail without him, Snag centered himself and turned to the second cell.

There was little question of what he would find inside.

He grasped the handle and the door swung open. Inside, Bael's chief minion awaited him, unruffled in his modern black suit and dark glasses, standing in the middle of the bare room with a dull-eyed, emaciated boy in his grip. A sword rested at the young vampire's throat. The child's mind hummed with unrealized power, held in check by his body's weakness and his own inexperience.

Snag knew what Eris believed about the boy, and he also knew that Eris was wrong. That knowledge made what he was about to do taste even bitterer than it would have otherwise—but he would do it nonetheless. One of the reasons Snag was a chess grandmaster was because he had learned that, in the end, the life of an innocent pawn was every bit as valuable as the life of a bishop, a knight, or a king.

He met Bastian Kovac's mirrored gaze impassively, and watched the slow smile spread across his undead face.

"Greetings, nightcrawler. Or perhaps I should call you Wolf Father instead?" said the puppet, his power rolling across the distance separating them to tangle with Snag's. Kovac laughed — an unpleasant sound — and continued. "No matter. Surrender yourself to my Master, or I will destroy the child."

The razor-sharp edge of the sword pressed harder against the boy's throat, tipping his head back. Behind him, Snag felt Eris register the words and jerk his head around, distracted from the opponent he was battling. An instant before the werewolf would have driven an iron blade through Eris' heart, Tré slammed into the undead creature, knocking it back a few steps.

I am sorry, my friend, Snag sent... the words for Eris alone. *You will understand why I did this in time.*

Blank incomprehension was his only reply, followed by shock as he silently walked into the cell. Oily black fog swirled up through the solid concrete of the floor, rising until it obscured all three of the cell's occupants. Snag closed his eyes as the old, well-remembered sensation of drowning in bitter acid overcame him. The last thing he heard was Eris' enraged cry echoing in his ears.

Fifteen

"*S*nag, *no!*" Eris roared, slashing viciously through his opponent's neck as Tré held its arms pinned. He didn't even wait to see the body fall before hurling himself toward the open cells, desperation and denial coursing through his veins in equal measure.

Bael was *here*. The demon's power was rising from the earth beneath them in a poisonous mist, and Eris could feel the others becoming aware of the hated creature's presence as they focused on their remaining opponents with renewed determination.

Snag had disappeared inside the cell without a backward glance, but as Eris neared the door, he turned. His dark eyes met Eris' gaze for only a moment before black fog billowed around the three figures inside, obscuring them. A burst of power— Snag's? Bael's?—slammed Eris backwards. He hit the floor hard. By the time he rolled to his feet and lunged forward again, the cell was empty except for a few rapidly dissipating wisps of darkness.

SNAG! he called mentally, channeling every bit of psychic power he possessed into the silent shout.

There was no reply.

-O-O-O-

Xander heard Eris mentally cry out Snag's name, but he couldn't afford to split his attention now that he finally had Crank cornered. Well, he had what was left of Crank cornered, at any rate—which, if he were being honest with himself, was nothing at all except for a very large, very hard to destroy hunk of muscle and bone.

Bael and Kovac had made sure of that.

The newly born wolf in him raged at the lost chance to extract any meaningful revenge on his rival, but the cold-hearted bastard of a vampire in him was content to take out his frustrations on whatever was left over.

Blood dripped from the fur of Xander's chest where an iron dagger had opened his flesh, but what would once have been debilitating agony was now merely an annoyance. Crank swiped at him with one meaty fist and he ducked under the blow, twisting to snap his jaws around the werewolf's hamstring. His opponent staggered and tried to shake him off, but his wolf was well acquainted with the struggling of larger prey. He jerked his head back and forth, widening the wound and attempting to drag Crank off balance.

The taste of dead flesh and blood made his nose wrinkle. A wolf might tolerate carrion when nothing better was available, but it was beyond sickening to a vampire. Nevertheless, Crank stumbled under his assault and went down on one knee. Xander abandoned his hold in favor of slamming his full weight into Crank's midsection. Beefy arms closed around his canine body in a punishing bear hug as he tried to get teeth near Crank's throat.

Not for the first time in the last few minutes, he wished he'd had more time to gain familiarity with this new form before being thrown directly into battle. Still, he could appreciate good design when he was walking around in it, and the wolf was definitely a killing machine. He wriggled, that tender throat almost within reach... even though it felt like his ribs were about to crack.

In the next instant, another set of canine jaws clamped around one of Crank's arms and pulled. *Manisha.* As he twisted free from Crank's hold, Xander caught a glimpse of her elegant form — slender with thick gray and white fur, blood coating her muzzle and chest. He knew in a deeper, more human part of himself that there would be serious emotional repercussions for such a sweet, gentle human when she shifted back... assuming they both survived the night. But he couldn't help his instinctive animal reaction to seeing her in battle, tearing fearlessly at the man who had wronged her so badly.

Xander lunged for Crank's jugular and started ripping. It wouldn't be enough to put the undead werewolf down for the count, he knew — but it still felt *really fucking good*. When Crank's throat was a torn and bloody mess, he went to work on the arm Manisha wasn't currently tearing to shreds and efficiently severed the ligaments.

Crank's legs continued to kick out, but Xander ignored them. Using his weight to pin the large figure, he took a moment to turn his focus inward, feeling out the shape of this new transformative ability. With an application of will, he flipped the mental switch controlling it, and an instant later, he knelt straddling Crank in human form.

A quick glance around located Tré, and he snapped, "Tré! *Blade!*" He pinned Crank with on forearm pressed to his ruined throat, and lifted his other hand as Tré met his eyes. A dagger arced toward him, hilt first, and he snatched it out of the air. Manisha shied away from the glint of silver, but he was too intent on ending the fight to react to her flinch.

The blade slashed through Crank's neck, and when it hit bone, Xander grabbed Crank's skull and *wrenched*. The feel of vertebra snapping made him grit his teeth. A moment later, the head hit the ground nearby and the body beneath him subsided into weak twitching. He rolled free and ran an appreciative thumb over the flat of the antique silver blade, only to hiss in surprise as the metal burned his skin.

"Oh, my god. Are you fucking joking?" he asked the knife, as the implication set in. *Great. One tiny little incident of exchanging bodily fluids with a werewolf and he was no longer sensitive to iron, but to silver instead. Bloody typical.*

He took stock, aware that the others were finishing up as well. Setting the traitorous knife safely out of reach of any twitching undead limbs, he turned to Manisha, who was still in wolf form, shaking Crank's unresponsive body by the arm like a rag doll.

"Manisha," he said, trying to modulate his voice to something reassuring rather than murderous. "Manisha, It's over. He's finished. Come away."

He wasn't entirely sure what to expect when his arms closed around her furry shoulders. She growled and gave the body a final shake, but relented under his grip and backed away. Christ, she truly was beautiful; gray-furred, golden-eyed, and with the tips of her ears as black as though they'd been dipped in ink. Her wide eyes darted around the basement, looking for additional threats and finding them all eliminated.

"That's right," he said, still trying to calm her. "Come back, Manisha. Come back to me now. You can do it — look inside yourself and remember what being human feels like. You changed outside of the full moon. That means you can control this. I know you can."

She shivered in his grip. For a long moment, nothing happened, but then the body under his hands twisted and he was holding her human form, shuddering and gasping.

"I've got you," he said, turning her so he could pull her against his chest. "All right. I've got you."

Xander knew something big must have happened while he and the others were focused on not getting killed by rampaging undead werewolves. He'd felt a dark, powerful presence that he'd never wanted to feel again, and then Eris had completely lost his shit, calling out for Snag. Xander could think of a handful of possible scenarios that would cover the facts, all of them equally bad. This much was certain, though — Bael's noxious, much-hated presence had retreated back to whatever rock it usually lived under. He couldn't sense it anymore. Nor could he feel any hint whatsoever of Bastian Kovac, or the child Sangye.

Or of Snag.

As if she'd heard the boy's name echo inside his mind, Manisha murmured, "*Sangye...*" against his chest, and tried to push upright.

He attempted to steady her, but she was already pulling free and staggering to her feet. "I need to get him out of those shackles!" she said, ignoring both her nakedness and the blood coating her face and neck. "We have to get him away from here—"

"Manisha," he warned, rising shakily to join her.

It was too late, though. She'd already stumbled over to the second cell door, catching herself against the frame in a pose that mirrored Eris'.

"No," she whispered. "No, he can't be gone... he was *here*. No, no *no*—"

Her voice rose, the denials growing louder. Xander closed his hands over her shoulders from behind.

"We'll figure out what happened and find them," he said firmly, hoping that the words wouldn't end up being yet another bullet point entry on the long list of promises to her that he hadn't been able to keep. "Eris?" he prodded.

But Eris was still staring blankly into the empty cell, his fingers clenching the doorframe so hard Xander was surprised he hadn't splintered it. The sound of a female throat being cleared behind him drew his attention away. He looked over his shoulder to find Della pointedly not looking at him as she proffered her knee-length black leather jacket in his general direction.

"Thanks," he said distractedly, taking the clothing and gently placing it over Manisha's shaking shoulders. She gripped it around herself, but her eyes never moved from the place where Sangye had been.

"Oy! Little Lord Fauntleroy. Incoming," warned Trynn. A pair of bloodstained trousers slapped against Xander's shoulder, and he scrambled to catch them. "Put those on. No one wants to see the view your flashing us right now."

It was a testament to how far down the shitter they'd already circled that it didn't seem worth the effort to toss out a comeback to the casual insult. But, on a more practical note, Trynn also had the best chance of anyone here at dragging information out of Eris right now — and they needed to know what the hell was going on.

He put on the damned trousers, trying to ignore the fact that they'd just been pulled off a dead werewolf.

"Eris," Trynn said, grasping her mate's shoulder and pulling him around to look at her. "Hey, now. What just happened? I can't feel Snag anymore. What did that crazy bastard do?"

Eris blinked, as if coming back to himself. He took a breath as if to speak, but nothing emerged. Tré joined them. "Tell us what you saw, Eris. *Quickly*," he ordered.

With a slow shake of his head, Eris met their eyes in turn — all except Manisha's, who was still staring at the empty iron shackles hanging from the back wall of the cell.

"He just... walked right into Bael's hands," he said, as if he couldn't conceive of Snag ever doing such a thing. As if it had been a personal betrayal.

In Eris' defense, Xander was at something of a loss as well. They'd all worried for a long time that Snag's sanity was... tenuous. But he'd seemed to be getting *better* recently, not worse. Xander could picture precisely zero circumstances under which he would voluntarily give himself over to Bael. It was utterly unthinkable. Death would be preferable.

Hell, eternal torture would be preferable.

"What about Sangye?" Manisha asked softly. "Kovac was with him in this cell. Where did they go? How could they have just... disappeared like this?"

Eris took a deep breath. "Kovac was holding a sword to the boy's neck. He ordered Snag to surrender himself to Bael, and Snag just... *did it*." His eyes flew to Tré's, flashing gold. "We have to find him and get him back. We can't let him do this."

Suddenly, Manisha was in Eris' face, her eyes glowing just as brightly. "*Them!*" she snarled. "We have to get *them* back! I don't know who this other person you're talking about is, and I don't really care! But don't you dare ignore Sangye! He's just an innocent boy, and I... I was supposed to..."

Her chest started to hitch beneath the words. Xander clasped her upper arms from behind, easing her back a few steps, out of Eris' personal space.

"I was supposed to protect him," she managed as she dissolved into tears. Aching for her, he turned her around and pressed her against him so that her next words were muffled against his shoulder. "I swore I'd protect him..."

Xander rested a hand on her head, smoothing his palm over her tangled hair and saying nothing — painfully familiar with the realities of letting down those you loved.

Tré's deep voice filled the silence that followed. "Eris. Can you sense Snag or Kovac at all right now? Is there any indication of where they might currently be?" he asked, taking effortless command of the situation as he always did.

"No," Eris said in a hollow voice. "They were here, and then they were gone. There's nothing."

"Very well," Tré said, all cold practicality. "We have injuries, and we're also far too exposed here in unfamiliar territory. We'll regroup at the Mayfair flat, contact the others in Singapore, and decide what to do from there."

It took a few minutes searching among the werewolves' personal belongings to find a stash of extra clothing that fit Manisha, and another that would do for Xander long enough for them to get back to his flat. Fortunately, aside from the slash across his chest, Xander hadn't fared too badly in the fight, and Manisha only had scrapes and bruises.

Tré had a stab wound in one thigh that didn't seem to have hit anything terribly vital. Eris sported a nasty slice down the length of his upper arm from shoulder to elbow.

Neither Trynn nor Della had suffered anything serious in the fight, and a taste of their blood was enough to start their mates' injuries healing. On the negative side, the iron blades meant that it would take more time and energy than usual for them to recover completely. Xander waved off Trynn's offered wrist, knowing the blood Snag had given him earlier would help him heal before long without any additional feeding—especially since his body no longer reacted violently to iron.

Della and Trynn flew ahead to ready the flat for their arrival while the rest of them followed by taxi. They weren't a particularly salubrious looking bunch by that point, but apparently the cabbie had seen worse in recent months. He ran a jaded eye over them and shrugged, driving them the five miles to Mayfair without comment... or the need for hypnotism.

Xander couldn't deny the way his shoulders relaxed in relief as he led Manisha into the sprawling penthouse flat, arming the security system behind them once the door was closed and locked. The stark, gleaming panorama of glass and metal was the closest thing he had to a home of his own, even if he'd only really stayed here during fleeting business visits to London over the past few years.

People told him the flat was elegant, but he knew it was actually cold—a reflection of himself, and the farthest thing he'd been able to find from dark, ornate Victorian sensibilities. Right now, though, it was undoubtedly a refuge. Nothing short of Bael himself could reach them in here without Xander knowing about it first, and they had everything they could possibly need. The place was outfitted and stocked with nothing but the best.

The familiar surroundings were more than welcome, because he was frankly a bit freaked out at this point by Manisha's continued air of utter defeat. She'd wept quietly on the drive over, neither encouraging Xander nor resisting him as he tucked her against his side and stroked her hair, murmuring soothing nonsense that he knew did her no good.

Now, she seemed wrung out, acceding to his guiding arm around her shoulders and showing no reaction to what was happening around her. In a human, he would have called it shock. In a newly-turned werewolf who had exchanged an alarming amount of blood with a vampire and then had her entire life ripped apart in front of her eyes, he didn't know what to call it beyond *bad*.

"Spiked blood is on the top shelf of the refrigerator hidden in the pantry," he told the others. "Un-spiked blood is on the second shelf. You know where the guest bathroom is; there are robes and some spare clothing in the hall closet. Manisha and I will be in the master suite. We might be a while. The Wi-Fi password is *G3t-off-my-LAN!*, but I'd rather you waited until we get back before you Skype the three musketeers in Singapore. It's mid-morning there anyway — they're probably asleep."

Tré nodded, his expression one of understanding. "Go. We're fine here. Take care of her, *tovarăş*."

Xander threw him a look of gratitude, and guided Manisha deeper into the flat on dragging feet. He knew there were a hundred things he should be focusing on—a thousand questions they needed answered—but right now, he couldn't spare a single thought for any of it.

He couldn't spare thought for anything except the woman in his arms.

SIXTEEN

The feeling of strong arms leading her slowly through an unfamiliar maze of rooms barely penetrated Manisha's cloak of misery. Her wolf wanted to howl—to cry out its pain to the world. She felt it urging her to shift again, and while a part of her wondered if the bitter loss of Sangye would hurt less if she gave into its demands, the larger part of her knew she would need her human wits to face whatever came next.

Right now, though, it was all she could do to face putting one foot in front of the other. Had it not been for Xander's grip on her shoulders, she was quite certain she would have sunk down into a pathetic heap on the floor and never moved again.

The conversation between the others had flowed over her, not really sticking, but she gathered they were somewhere the vampires considered safe, at least for now. The pristine, tastefully staged surroundings could not have been more different from the grungy warehouse basement with its converted holding cells, mouse-infested walls, and overflowing toilet.

After rattling off the string of instructions to his friends, Xander had been silent as he led her deeper into the elegant apartment. They passed through a bedroom with a king-sized bed decked out in black, white, and dove gray. She had a brief impression of expensive modern art hanging on the walls.

Double doors led into a spacious bathroom arranged around the centerpiece of a huge, clear glass walk-in shower. He guided her to the far wall and settled her down on the closed lid of the toilet, kneeling in front of her. His hands closed around hers, squeezing. She stared down at their tangled fingers, her gaze unfocused… and *ached* for everything she'd lost.

"Manisha," he said, in that low, velvet-wrapped voice, "look at me. You're safe now. Nothing will happen to you here."

She lifted her eyes until they met his moss-green gaze. His brows drew together.

"Do you trust me?" he asked.

The silence stretched, and finally her muddled brain realized that he was waiting for her to answer the question. Did she trust him?

He had come for her. In fact, he'd done every single thing she'd asked of him. She'd slapped him… attempted to throttle him in the throes of bloodlust… practically *raped* him—and he'd still risked his life to try to save her and Sangye.

A callused hand cradled her cheek. "Stop," he said. "Look—I'll concede the slap and the attempted strangulation, but you did *not* 'practically rape' me. I'll grant you, it wasn't the most carefully negotiated BDSM scene I've ever participated in. For once, though, I was the sober one in the equation—so I think you've got more room for complaint there than I do. Now, answer the question, Manisha."

She had to think for a moment to remember what she was supposed to be answering. "I trust you," she whispered.

Some of the tension in his bearing drained away. "Good."

"How did you know what I was thinking just now?" she asked, though the question emerged flat. "And before, when I thought I heard you in my head in the warehouse."

"We're two dark creatures who have shared each others' blood," he answered without hesitation. "It's a bit spotty right now, admittedly, but that means there's a mental bond between us. Look inside yourself. Can you feel it?"

She tried to look inside herself, but there was only emptiness. She shook her head slowly.

"I don't know what to do now," she said in a hollow tone. "What do I do now?"

The hollowness flowed down into her stomach, making it cramp.

"Now, we get you cleaned up," Xander told her firmly. "Or rather, we'll get both of us cleaned up, I suppose... but you first." He lifted her hand and pressed a kiss to her knuckles before settling it in her lap and rising. She watched him move around the bathroom, setting out clean towels and starting the water running in the cavernous shower.

With a sudden jolt, she realized that she hadn't had a hot shower in *weeks*. Without giving it another thought, she started pulling off the ill-fitting, borrowed clothes Xander's friends had found for her and tossing them away. She was shuffling out of the threadbare leggings when Xander turned back to her. He paused, but didn't look away or blush. After a brief flicker downwards, he focused his gaze squarely on her face and moved toward her as if to assist her.

Tired of feeling helpless, she ignored his outstretched hand, only for her knees to give way the moment she stood and tried to take a step under her own power. He was there before she could hit the ground, catching her and keeping her upright.

"Let me help," he said quietly. "Unless you'd rather shift—it'd be easier to stay upright on four legs than two, I imagine. And I can always clean the dog hair out of the shower drain later."

She shook her head and let him support her over to the shower. Steam billowed out as he swung the door open on silent hinges. He didn't remove his own clothing beyond toeing off the too-large, borrowed boots; he just half-walked and half-carried her into the warm spray of water, ignoring the way it soaked the ratty t-shirt and military-style khakis he'd taken from the warehouse.

The stinging spray of droplets against her filthy, blood-encrusted skin was like nirvana. Her knees crumpled again, but rather than holding her upright, Xander controlled their descent until they were both sitting against the glass wall. She turned into him, all of her pride and self-respect apparently having fled the moment she saw the empty cell where Sangye should have been.

As he had done before, Xander sheltered her against his body without a word. She let her long hair fall over her face like a curtain. He rubbed a hand along her spine with long, sure strokes as the hot water pelted her, driving back the chill that had settled over her soul.

Evidently, the wolf lived too firmly in the moment to hold onto that much hurt when her mate's arms were around her and his lips were pressed against the crown of her head. The animal slowly settled, even as Manisha's human mind continued to worry at the feelings of grief and failure.

"Shh," Xander said. "Listen to the wolf on this one. Let it all go for a few minutes and just rest. I'll hold onto it for you in the mean time—I promise. We're not abandoning them. We're just regrouping."

Manisha still wasn't sure how to feel about the idea of him being able to see her thoughts—though at least it saved her the energy of trying to talk right now. This time, when she looked inside herself, she thought she could almost feel the sense of him inside her mind. A cool, reflective surface, hiding troubled depths beneath.

"All right," she murmured against his skin, watching through a gap in her hair as the rivulets of water running toward the drain turned slowly from rusty brown to clear.

It was such a relief to set everything aside for a little while. To simply exist, here in this warm, steamy haven with strong arms holding her. She drifted for what seemed like a very long time, though the water showed no signs of cooling. Xander stretched out an arm, reaching for something,

161

and a moment later a soft cloth lathered soap over her skin as he scrubbed at her gently.

She let him work without reacting except to move this way and that as he guided her around so he could reach all of her. His touch was thorough without being salacious, and the wolf rumbled in satisfaction under the casual intimacy of the situation. By the time the last of the grime was gone from her skin, there wasn't an ounce of tension left in her muscles. He tucked her soaking hair behind her ear and stroked her cheek with his fingertips, coaxing her eyes to open and meet his.

"Back with me now?" he asked, trying on a brief twitch of a smile that didn't manage to cover the rather lost expression lurking behind his gaze.

She blinked, not quite ready to face what awaited them beyond the steamy glass walls.

"There's... uh... there's some shampoo here if you want it. And conditioner," he said. "If you're all right on your own for a minute, I should give myself a quick scrub, too. Unless, you know, you'd rather I help you out so you can get dried off first. You could lie down for a bit while I—"

"No," she said, her voice emerging raspy. "Go on. I'm fine right here."

Fine maybe wasn't the word. Her stomach was cramping again, a strange, gnawing sensation that grew worse as he nodded his understanding and helped her prop herself against the wall, the shampoo and conditioner bottles within easy reach. When he straightened away, moving to the other end of the large space and turning his back, that strange hunger pressed her to get up and follow him.

She pushed down the impulse and tried to focus on washing her filthy, tangled hair. Still, she couldn't help sending glances his way as he pulled off the soaked black t-shirt, revealing the rippling muscles of his back. He reached up and turned on a second showerhead, then set to work efficiently washing himself as best he could with the ill-fitting trousers still hanging low on his hips.

Feeling slightly revived, she rinsed her hair and worked conditioner into it, picking through the worst of the tangles with her fingers while trying to ignore the empty hole yawning in her stomach.

The wolf grumbled, discontent.

-o-o-o-

Xander steeled himself to turn around again. It was a kind of torture, having Manisha here like this. Caring for her, as though he had some right to this intimacy with a woman whose life he had destroyed not once, but twice now.

How did he expect to be able to help her find Sangye when the boy had not only been whisked away without a trace, but had been whisked away by *Bael himself*? It appeared now that not even Snag could stand against the demon's power. And if Snag couldn't resist, the rest of them had about as much chance in this fight as a snowball had in hell.

He shoved the thoughts aside and let the spray run over his face, washing everything away. When he blinked the water out of his eyes and turned around, it was to find Manisha standing only a step away from him. His brows drew together — he hadn't even heard her move.

She looked frighteningly pale beneath her rich olive complexion, and her eyes were fevered. He tried to get a sense of her through the faint connection running between them, only to be hit with the echo of a strong spasm that nearly doubled her over. His hands shot out to steady her, a fresh stab of fear piercing him.

Was she hurt? Ill? It had almost felt like —

She clutched at her stomach, grimacing up at him. "Please… something's wrong. I n-need — "

Understanding flooded him, and he gripped her shoulders harder.

"Blood," he said. "Oh, my god. I drained you, and you bit me. And now you're craving blood."

Her eyes glowed yellow. "It hurts," she whispered. "I — I can't…"

He didn't even think. He pulled her flush against his body, bending down a bit so that her lips brushed the juncture of his neck and shoulder. She gasped and tried to twist her head away, but he lifted a hand to the back of her head.

"*Manisha*," he said. "Drink. You've been fighting the cravings for a while now, haven't you? You're weak. You need blood. Christ… why didn't I realize — ?"

She made a broken noise and an instant later, sharp teeth pierced his neck. His eyes slipped closed as she drew his blood inside herself, and he struggled to keep his traitorous cock under control. *Not the time*, he told himself firmly. Even so, he thought a moan might've slipped free... or maybe that had only been in his head.

Because the bond between them was flaring into life now, a supernova compared to the dim little dwarf star he'd glimpsed earlier.

What am I doing so good no no mustn't no stop need you so much please please no I can't be alone like this anymore what's wrong with me – ?

Manisha. Enough, he told her. *You're not alone anymore. Can you feel me in your mind now?*

A thread of surprise wove through her growing hysteria. *What? How –*

He stroked his fingers over the wet, heavy mass of her hair. The fangs buried in his neck sank deeper, and the strong pull of her mouth against his flesh might as well have been reaching down the length of his body to tug directly on his balls.

He struggled to keep that fact from coloring his voice as he said, "I told you. We shared blood. Now you're strengthening the link even more."

I asked you not to let me hurt you! she raged, even as her body latched on more tightly to his. *I practically begged you! I can't control what I'm doing –*

A lovely, light-headed feeling was beginning to wash over him – one that he suspected would be utterly sublime to experience while his cock was buried inside her to the hilt.

No, Xander, he reminded himself. *Bad vampire. Down, boy.*

He huffed a breath that might have been self-deprecating laughter. "You can't hurt me by draining my blood, love. I'm a vampire. If I pass out on you, just nip into the kitchen and grab a bottle of red from the fridge. Pour it down my throat and I'll be good as new afterward — promise."

He swallowed, feeling the movement of her fangs against his flesh as his throat bobbed. *And if you think this is hurting me,* he added, *you're not paying close enough attention to the link.*

He felt her focus turn further inward. He could tell the moment when she truly felt him — felt his body's response — rather than merely hearing his words. She jerked away from him with a gasp of surprise, leaving him reeling a bit at the sudden loss. Steadying himself with a hand against the glass enclosure, he blinked at her through the spray of hot water, watching as she tried to file this new bit of information in with all the other things whirling around in her head like a file cabinet full of papers caught in a hurricane.

"You don't have to stop, you know," he said. "Not until the cravings are sated. Unless you'd rather I went and got you a bottle to drink from instead of a vein?"

She was breathing hard, and it was a considerable struggle to keep his eyes on her face rather than watching the way rivulets of water trickled down the golden-brown expanse of her heaving breasts. It became even harder when he noticed the way her eyes were tracing the path of the blood trickling from his neck as it mixed with the shower water and ran down his chest.

Manisha lifted fingertips to her bottom lip, dabbing at the smear of his blood that clung there. He found he couldn't look away from the glistening red mark.

"I, um... no. I think..." She paused, sucking the last traces of blood from her lip. Xander could see that her teeth were once again human-flat as she continued, "I think I'm all right now. In fact, I don't feel nearly as weak and out-of-it as I did before. What's happening to me?"

"The same thing that's happening to me, I gather," he said. "Only in reverse. We need to talk to the others. As far as I know, a werewolf has never bitten a vampire before. Or vice versa."

She pressed the heel of her hand to her forehead as if fighting a headache. "This is crazy," she muttered.

He quirked an eyebrow. "Yes. Welcome to my world."

Manisha shook her head. A moment later, she seemed to take in her surroundings properly for the first time since they had arrived at the flat. Her cheeks darkened.

He tore his eyes away from her with difficulty. "I'll get you a towel and a robe," he said. "Stay here. I won't be a minute."

Xander slipped out of the shower before he could talk himself into staying, and closed the door behind him. The glass walls were covered with steam, blocking her view, so he stripped off the borrowed trousers and tossed them into the Japanese soaking tub set against the side wall. After drying off and donning a robe, he took a towel from the warming rack and draped a second robe over his arm.

Rapping his knuckles lightly on the outside of the glass, he waited for the water to turn off and the door to swing open partway so he could hand the towel to her without looking. Then he hung the robe from the corner of the open shower door.

"There's a comb on the vanity," he said. "Clean toothbrushes in the top left drawer under the sink. Help yourself to anything in the flat, and if you can't find something, ask. I'll be right outside. When you're done, we'll go speak with the others and figure out our next move."

Call me if you need anything, he added, and left before she could formulate any kind of an answer, either silently or aloud.

Xander closed the bathroom door and leaned back against it, putting up enough of a mental shield to hide his thoughts from her while still ensuring that he would feel it if she was in any distress.

Bloody, buggering hell. Where did he get off thinking he had the right to treat her like this—to treat her as if she was his? She didn't know the first thing about him; had no reason to trust him and every reason not to.

He pushed away from the door, and the resulting mild dizziness catapulted his mind right back to the feeling of her fangs piercing him, her lips pressing against the tender skin of his throat as she drank him down. For a vampire, it was foreplay, but for her, it was probably some serious horror movie shit—another nightmare come to life. And that *still* completely ignored the fact that he had no real idea what the two of them had done to each other.

It appeared he was now a vampire who could survive direct sunlight, but shifted into the form of a wolf instead of mist or an owl, and was burned by silver. While she was a werewolf who craved blood and could change her form outside of the full moon. It made no sense. And it also made perfect sense.

He dressed quickly, unwilling to face the others without donning at least the appearance of his usual armor beforehand. Manisha emerged into the bedroom a short time later, the robe tied snugly around her body and her damp hair plaited in a messy braid that hung nearly to her waist. Xander wanted to run his fingers through that long, silky hair. He wanted to see what it looked like spread across a pillow like a dark halo. He wanted to erase that hollow, haunted look from her eyes.

He was so, *so* fucked.

"I can try and find you some clothes that fit," he offered.

"Will we be leaving here tonight?" she asked.

He shook his head. "I shouldn't think so. Like Tré said, we need to regroup and decide what we're going to do before we run off half-cocked."

"Then the robe is fine," she said. Silence stretched, and it seemed she was deciding whether or not to say something else. "Do you think Sangye is dead?" she asked eventually, the words emerging all in a rush.

He shook his head. "No. I don't."

She examined his face for a long moment. "Are you just saying that to keep from upsetting me?"

He stepped into her space so he could look down at her, not even aware that he was doing it until he'd already moved. "Not at all." He paused, trying to organize his thoughts into words. "Bael turned Sangye *purposely*. He's never done that before. The rest of us... we were his mistakes. His goal these past long years has been to destroy vampires, not add to our ranks. He must have had a reason for that."

Her eyebrows drew together, a furrow forming in the skin between them. "Bael? Is that the name of Kovac's master? The ancient evil he serves?"

The vitriolic burn of Xander's hatred coiled in his gut. "Yes. The demon that tried to make us into his soulless puppets, and instead turned us into what we are now. You may have seen dark mist swirling around Snag and Sangye when they were taken. That mist is the physical manifestation of his power."

Her eyes slipped closed. "That's what destroyed the werewolves and made them into undead... *things*. I felt it touch me. It was like acid; I thought I was going to die."

The thought of Bael touching the woman standing before him was like a stake through his chest. His hands closed around her arms, startling her into looking up at him again.

"We're devoted to stopping him, Manisha—no matter what it takes," he said hoarsely. "Bael's defeat is our one and only purpose in life. I'm just sorry you got caught up in it."

Her lips pressed together in a firm line. "Until this happened, I had never before in my life felt the desire to kill someone."

Xander's shields slipped, and for a moment he felt their mutual hatred of Bael flow together like blood and water mixing.

"I have a feeling it won't be as straightforward as simple killing," he said. "But whatever happens, you are one of us now. So is Sangye—and we look after our own. You're not alone in this. We're all in it together, to the bitter end."

She took a deep breath and let it out. "Let's go talk to the others."

Seventeen

Manisha followed Xander back to the flat's spacious sitting room, the floor smooth and warm under her bare feet. Not surprisingly, the others had gotten themselves cleaned up while she was busy having a meltdown in Xander's luxurious shower.

She looked at the other vampires properly for the first time — two couples, all four of them strikingly attractive in different ways. One of the men was pale-skinned, with high Slavic cheekbones, a serious brow, and unusual silver-gray eyes beneath dark hair. Next to him sat a woman about Manisha's height or a bit shorter, with a riot of wavy chestnut hair and the sort of curves that would make any man look twice.

Another woman sat cross-legged on a second couch. Her black hair was close cropped at the sides with a longer forelock falling across her forehead. She was taller and built a bit boyishly, though her full lips and the delicate brows arched over her intelligent eyes still marked her as a very striking woman.

A second man — the one Manisha vaguely remembered yelling at earlier — paced restlessly around the open, airy space. Dark, wavy hair on the long side of fashionable framed sharply drawn

Mediterranean features. His brown eyes were flat and angry.

Xander ushered her further into the room, and all four vampires looked at her.

"Manisha," Xander said, "may I present Della, Tré, Eris, and Trynn. Try not to hold their long history of voluntary association with me against them."

Tré rose, and offered a precise bow of the head that you might expect to see from old world aristocracy in a movie. "A pleasure," he said in a deep, Eastern European accent.

The woman named Della rose as well, and came forward to clasp Manisha's hand in a brief handshake. "Hi," she said, her voice a broad American drawl. "It's nice to meet you."

"Horrible circumstances notwithstanding, of course. Unfortunately, we tend to get those a lot," added the dark-haired woman, Trynn. Rather than rise and shake Manisha's hand, she smiled tightly and gestured to another of the elegant couches scattered around the large space. "Make yourself comfortable. I expect we've got quite a bit to discuss."

"That we do," said the other man—Eris. His tone was grim. She thought maybe he was Greek, but mostly what struck her was the aura of age and barely leashed power crackling around him like invisible sparks.

It made the wolf restless and put Manisha on edge, but she only nodded and said, "All right," before taking a seat on the empty couch Trynn had indicated.

Xander followed her and sank down to sit on the floor near her legs, bracing his back against the edge of the couch and stretching. She heard a series of pops as his spine cracked, and he relaxed into a slouch, close to her but not touching. Tré and Della returned to their previous seats, while Eris circled around to stand behind Trynn and rest his hands on the back of the sofa, still looking twitchy.

"Before we get into the rest of it," Xander said, "I need to pick your brains on something."

"Oh? You mean the small matter of you being impervious to sunlight and unexpectedly shifting into a wolf?" Eris asked. "I was wondering when you'd ask."

Manisha felt a glimmer of irritation that didn't belong to her pricking inside her head. That mental link... was going to take some serious getting used to. It had implications that she wasn't quite ready to examine too closely.

"Manisha bit me while she was in mid-transformation," Xander said very precisely, clipping the words off one at a time, "and I bit her in an attempt to weaken her enough that she could assert her humanity over the wolf. There was a fairly significant exchange of... bodily fluids... and we both became quite ill afterward."

Eris muttered something in a language Manisha didn't recognize. Xander lifted his chin, but didn't move from his loose sprawl otherwise.

"Eris, mate," he said, "I get that your knickers are in a twist over Snag. But right now, I need a peek into that encyclopedia you keep locked up inside your two-thousand-year-old skull. I do *not*—

" He paused, emphasizing the word. " —need you judging me under your breath in Cypriot. Which I do, in fact, speak."

Della was frowning. "Wait. So, you think that by sharing Manisha's blood, you've become... what? Part werewolf?"

"That's what I'm hoping the bookworm can answer," Xander said. "Though it's not just me that's affected, it's both of us."

Eris' dark eyes flicked over them, a hint of gold lurking behind them. "Tell me exactly what you've both experienced since then."

Xander gestured at her in a clear *ladies first* gesture.

Manisha cleared her throat, looking around at the interested gazes nervously. "It was right after my first transformation. The moon was setting, and Xander got close to me too soon. I... uh... I attacked him. When I came back to myself properly, I felt really dizzy and weak. I must've passed out. The werewolves took me back to the warehouse and chained me up with what I'm pretty sure were silver shackles."

"Did the metal burn your skin?" Eris asked, all business now.

She nodded. "Yes, it was awful. After I woke up, they brought me some meat. I was ravenous, and after I ate it I felt a bit stronger. But... there was also blood on my skin, and I wanted to lick it off. I remember thinking that fresh blood would have been even better."

Eris' eyebrows went up. "So you wanted both food and blood? And the meat didn't make you feel ill?"

"Yes, I wanted both," she said. "And, no, eating didn't make me feel sick."

"Are you still craving blood?" Eris asked.

Manisha felt her cheeks heat, and shot a glance at the top of Xander's head.

"She was craving it, yes," Xander said evenly. "She's not anymore."

His fingers reached up to brush the side of his neck, where Manisha could just make out red marks and bruising. The others' attention focused on the movement, and Eris nodded.

"Right," he said. "Xander, have you tried eating solid food?"

Xander made a vague noise of disgust. "No, I have not. Unlike Oksana, I don't enjoy putting my body through that. Speaking of which, we should Skype the Singapore brigade now so we don't have to go over the ugly details of this debacle twice."

Tré spoke up. "I'll do that. Are your passwords still the same?"

"Yes."

Tré made a noise of disapproval. "Your IT division would be appalled, *tovarăș*." He left the room and returned a moment later with a sleek laptop. "While I set up the call, you should check to see if you can tolerate human food now. I assume you have some around for… visitors?"

Something about the way he said it, combined with what Manisha thought she knew of Xander, made her think he was looking for a polite way to say *one-night stands*. Which should not have made her hackles rise, but did anyway.

Xander grunted and pushed to his feet. "Yeah, I think there's some microwave chicken tikka masala in the freezer."

"Classy," Trynn observed.

"Shut up," Xander told her.

Trynn snorted. Manisha's stomach rumbled audibly.

The corner of Xander's mouth twitched before his gaze landed on her, and softened. "Hungry again? I can heat up two portions."

She looked down. "I'm a vegetarian," she said bitterly. "Or at least, I was. But all the werewolves gave me after I was turned was meat. Most of which was fucking *raw*."

Della made a noise of combined sympathy and anger.

"Jesus," said Trynn. "What a bunch of bastards. Eris, does she have to eat meat just because she's a werewolf?"

Manisha raised her head to look at Trynn's mate, who lifted one shoulder in a shrug. "I've no idea, though I expect the wolf will dictate at least some of her physical requirements." His dark eyes met hers. "What are your feelings about fish and shellfish? Or about hunting small game while in the form of the wolf?"

She mulled it over for a few moments. "I'm not sure. Though I suppose I find the idea of eating shellfish is a bit less upsetting than gnawing on something's leg bone." She shuddered. "Or of pouncing on some poor, unsuspecting rabbit and breaking its neck in my jaws."

Della shifted position. "You know, the last Dalai Lama wasn't totally vegetarian. I remember reading that in an interview."

Manisha tried to smile at her despite the pang that went through her at the reminder of Sangye. "Yes. I know. Lots of Tibetan Buddhists aren't. Differing schools of thought. It's how I was raised, though."

"I'm fairly sure there's some pasta with scallops in the freezer, along with the chicken," Xander said. "I can at least offer you protein without a central nervous system. We can experiment more with your diet when you're not quite so busy recovering from... well... everything."

'*We* can experiment.' It should have sounded presumptuous. So why did the words make her wolf want to roll over and rub her back all over Xander's plush area rug?

"Okay. Thanks," she said. When he'd disappeared into the kitchen, she took a deep breath. "So, I'm really the first werewolf to bite a vampire? Or, you know, vice versa? Bully for me, I guess."

Eris arched a heavy eyebrow, his already dark expression hardening even further. "Well... yes and no," he said.

"Oh, *come on*, Eris! What the bloody hell is that supposed to mean?" Xander called from the kitchen, the ding of a microwave being set following the words.

"Let's wait for the Singapore call to go through, and get the others up to speed," Eris said. "I only want to tell this once."

A few moments later, Tré set the laptop on the coffee table facing the largest of the couches. The others clustered around it, and after a quick round of greetings with the newcomers, Tré ran through a succinct recap of recent events. Manisha crept around until she could see the screen, where a pretty black woman and a pale-skinned blonde who looked like a runway model sat with a pleasant-faced white man with sandy brown hair and blue eyes.

The microwave dinged again, and Xander emerged with two steaming plastic trays and a couple of elegant silver forks. She eyed the forks warily.

"It's stainless, not the good silver," he assured her, handing her one along with the tray of pasta. The food smelled ridiculously good for something that had just been removed from a cardboard box and microwaved.

Xander perched himself on the arm of the sofa, within range of the laptop's camera.

"Xander. We leave you alone for *one week*, mon chou…" said the blonde woman.

"Hello to you, too, Duchess," Xander said, and lifted a forkful of chicken to his nose. He winced, but gamely took a tiny taste.

And immediately spat it out.

"Problem?" asked the black woman. "And here I thought you might finally have seen the light."

"Yeah, that's a great big *no*," he said, and took the tray back into the kitchen.

Manisha dug into her pasta, the wolf seeming quite content with both the scallops and the creamy noodles with bits of broccoli mixed in.

"So," Xander continued upon returning, "not a completely equal exchange of characteristics, then."

The man on the laptop screen tapped his chin for a moment before speaking in a pleasant Australian accent. "That makes sense, though. Scientifically speaking, grafting werewolf abilities onto a vampire wouldn't necessarily have the same results as grafting vampire abilities onto a werewolf."

"Cheers, Ozzie," said Xander, "and kudos for being able to say both 'vampires' and 'werewolves' in the same sentence without flinching. I'm impressed."

"I'm a quick learner," the man replied in a dry tone.

"Strictly speaking," Eris said in a low voice, "they're all vampire traits, originally."

Xander crossed his arms. "Okay, enough. You seem to think the whole 'being cryptic' thing makes you look cool, and it really, *really* doesn't. You've been hinting around something all evening, and it's driving me batty. Which, I hasten to add, is neither a vampire nor a werewolf trait—thank you *so* much, Bram Stoker."

Manisha was starting to understand that engaging in endless quips was Xander's way of dealing with things that were unpleasant or emotional. Even though she couldn't feel the strange mental bond with him at all right now, she got the sense that he was rattled, and that, in turn, made *her* feel rattled.

Eris straightened from where he'd been leaning his hands on the back of the sofa. "To explain," he said, "I'm going to need to break a confidence."

The blonde woman on the laptop screen tilted her head like a bird. "Why? Is this to do with Snag?" she asked.

Trynn craned around to look at her mate with interest. "Is it?"

"It is, yes," Eris said. "Under the circumstances, it's directly relevant. And it's not as though he's here for me to ask permission." His voice grew tight on the last sentence.

EIGHTEEN

Eris turned to look at Manisha. "Snag is the oldest vampire in existence. The first vampire Bael ever made, unless another exists that we haven't found, or who was killed before the rest of us were turned. He was born in Egypt, south of what is now Cairo, in the year 2650 BCE or thereabouts — as far as I've been able to determine, at any rate. Snag has no knowledge of, or real interest in, his exact age."

Manisha tried to rein in her shock, even as Tré looked at Eris curiously.

"How do you know all of this?" the silver-eyed vampire asked. "In the centuries I've known him, I have never heard him speak of his past in any detail."

Trynn crossed her arms and glared at Tré. "Yeah? You know, if the rest of you talked to him more and didn't treat him like some kind of a freak, maybe he'd open up more to you in turn."

"He is a freak, Trynn," Xander said evenly. "We're all freaks, here — some of us more than others. And, I'm sorry, but Snag has always been firmly on the 'more' end of the spectrum."

Trynn inhaled as if to argue, but Eris spoke first.

"I know these things about Snag because I'm the one who stumbled across his petrified body in an underground tomb in 326 AD. And, yes, because I made the effort to cultivate his friendship over the course of the intervening centuries."

His expression darkened again, but he shook it off.

"He has always been different than the rest of us. More powerful. But also, more... damaged. He won't speak of what happened when he was turned. However, what the rest of you may not appreciate is that, in the almost forty-seven hundred years since he emerged from his initial bloodlust, he never once fed from a human until the day a few months ago when he helped me turn Trynn."

Trynn's eyes flew to her mate in surprise, and Eris rested a hand on her shoulder. A shocked silence settled across the room.

Manisha wasn't clear about what this had to do with werewolves, or with her and Xander, but it was undeniably difficult to take in. "If he's a vampire, and he's more than four thousand years old but has never hunted humans... how is he still alive?" she asked.

"He fed from Eris," Tré said slowly, "but only barely enough to keep himself functioning. More recently, he has fed from Trynn as well."

"Mostly because I never stopped nagging him about it," Trynn put in.

"However, that does not account for the almost three millennia after he was turned, but before you found him, Eris," Tré continued. "It seems unlikely that he could have survived that long without any blood whatsoever."

"I didn't say he survived without blood—although he did spend much of that period in a petrified, coma-like state brought on by starvation. That was how I found him, and he had been sealed inside his tomb for a very long time."

Xander tensed beside her. "But you said…"

"I said," Eris continued, "that he never fed from a human."

"Son of a bitch," Xander said. "This had better not be heading where I think it's heading, Eris."

Eris only stared at him.

"Go on," Tré prompted.

Eris let out a deep breath. "Snag ruled a minor city-state, and was something of a gadfly to the pharaoh at the time. After he was turned, several of Snag's former soldiers managed to subdue him and drag him before the priests while he was still weakened. The priests performed powerful spells on him to keep him that way."

The black woman on the laptop screen inhaled sharply. "Those scars on his body," she said, "some of them are symbols of power common across several ancient religions."

"Yes," Eris agreed. "The priests weakened him enough that he was unable to overpower them or shift form. Then, his former subjects presented him as a gift to the pharaoh, hoping to curry favor and avoid war now that they were leaderless. The pharaoh was happy enough to have his old adversary as a prisoner, and amused himself for several years by putting Snag in the arena with wild animals as a sort of spectacle."

The others looked grim. Della looked positively ill.

"Oh my god," she breathed. "He killed the animals and drank from them?"

"Rather than attack humans, yes," Eris said.

"The first time I saw him," Della said faintly, "I noticed that some of his scars looked like branded symbols, and the rest looked like—"

"Claw marks," Trynn finished for her, wincing. "Yeah. *Fuck.*"

Manisha thought she had a pretty good idea where this was going now.

Eris continued, "They threw him in with anything they could find that had fangs, claws, and a vicious temper. There was usually enough blood shed on both sides to entertain the crowds, but of course none of the animals could overcome him. He always killed them in the end. At least... he killed them until one day when the arena guards dragged a huge golden wolf out of the fighting pit, only to discover that it was stunned rather than dead."

"He drank from a wolf, but didn't kill it," Xander said flatly. "And... let me guess..."

Eris nodded. "It had bitten him, as well. The beast woke up and savaged one of the guards before escaping. A few days later, it started coming into the city at night, attacking people until someone finally managed to chop its head off."

"And those people it attacked turned into werewolves," Manisha said, feeling as ill as Della looked. "He *made* werewolves. By accident."

"As you say." Eris rubbed at the bridge of his nose. "After one of the surviving guards came in to throw the wolf's head at his feet and tell him what happened, Snag just... gave up. He stopped feeding at all; let the animals maul him until it wasn't enough of a show for the pharaoh's taste anymore. When he finally grew too weak to heal, he lapsed into a death-like state and his enemies sealed him in an underground tomb."

"And that's where you found him," Xander said flatly. "Three thousand years later."

"A human would have assumed he was a mummy," Eris said. "But even after all that time, I could still sense him inside my mind. It was the moment when I first discovered that I was not alone in the world."

Manisha shivered, imagining what it would be like to believe you were the only one of your kind in existence.

"How does any of this help, though?" she asked. "This vampire... this being who is responsible for making me what I am... is trapped somewhere with Sangye and a demon who wants us all dead. So now what?"

She rubbed her temples, wishing she could stop the pounding in her head somehow. After a few moments, she let her arms fall to her sides, a hollow laugh escaping her. "This is nuts. And you want to know what's even more ironic?"

Xander looked at her, concern lurking behind his green eyes.

"Sangye also refused to drink human blood," she continued. "At least... afterward. I can't say it for certain, but I'm fairly sure he must have killed his mother in the bloodlust right after he was, uh, changed."

"It is likely," Tré said in a heavy voice. "It's the willing sacrifice of a loved one's life that thwarts Bael's power, making his intended victim into a vampire rather than an undead puppet."

She nodded, thinking of Eliza Grimshaw, Xander's wife. About the woman Manisha had once been. "Jampa—Sangye's mother—would have given her life for him in a heartbeat. Of that, I have no doubt."

Manisha closed her eyes, remembering Sangye's monstrous demeanor as he'd snapped his jaws at her in a mindless killing frenzy, held back from ripping out her throat only by the iron chains shackling him.

She continued, "After they threw us into the cells at the warehouse, he seemed to come back to himself. And from that moment forward, he refused to feed even when Crank dangled bound humans right in front of his face." Tears began to burn behind her eyes, and she tried to blink them back. "The bastard tried everything he could think of. Cutting their flesh and waving the blood right under Sangye's nose... threatening to torture or murder them if he wouldn't feed."

An arm closed around her shoulders, but she kept staring forward blankly, her vision starting to blur.

"But... Sangye would just look at Crank in that quiet way he had, and tell him that he couldn't stop Crank from committing whatever violence he was intent on. And when the homeless kids Crank brought in for him started to panic or scream or cry, he'd meet their gaze, and his eyes would start to glow. He'd tell them not to be afraid; to go to sleep and that everything would be all right. And... they would do it. They would do exactly what he said."

She realized that her voice was shaking, and tears were sliding down her cheeks. The arm held her tighter.

"Xander, mate —" The Australian voice came from the laptop speakers, calm and sober. " — your lady friend needs someplace quiet, a shoulder to lean on, and a few hours' sleep. Doctor's orders."

"On it," said the quiet voice at her side.

"We still need to come up with a strategy —" Eris began.

Tré cut him off. "We need to rest and heal. Right now, we have no information to work with. Unless you can sense Snag's location?"

Eris' spine stiffened. Trynn looked up at him and said, "What if you tried to, I don't know... meditate for a bit first? Clear your mind, and then try to contact him again? Maybe the two of us together could do it."

Xander led Manisha away before she could hear Eris' response, heading back down the hallway to the luxurious master suite. She let herself be guided, suddenly feeling exhausted beyond measure. She was still crying, and the prospect of giving in fully to the wracking sobs that wanted to shake free of her chest was more than she could bear right now. She just wanted it all to go away for a bit. She needed… not to feel like this. She needed that desperately.

The bedroom door closed behind them, and Xander turned her so she was facing him, his hands bracketing her shoulders. She felt the barrier he'd erected earlier in his mind slide lower, his thoughts brushing up against hers as if to assess her state of mind.

"I'm going to make a suggestion," he said, "which you are free to ignore. In a minute, I'm going to shift into my wolf for a while. I think things will be easier for you if you do the same. Animals are… simpler, in many ways. Curl up on the bed. Sleep for a bit. Shed on the comforter and give my housekeeping service something to wonder about the next time they come. I'll keep watch and wake you if anything important happens."

She blinked up at him stupidly, but he only leaned down to press his lips to her forehead before letting her go and slipping into the bathroom. A moment later, the huge male wolf who'd fought at her side in the warehouse padded out, its green eyes full of depths she couldn't bring herself to plumb right now.

It sat at her feet, obviously ready to stand guard just as Xander had promised. The animal sharing Manisha's body and mind surged up, suddenly desperate to get free. To get to its mate. Fresh tears fell. How had all of this just… *happened*? The wolf was an entirely new part of her, appearing from nowhere like a puzzle piece that needed to be slotted into place before she could be whole again.

And she had no idea how to do that.

She hadn't asked for this. But what was the alternative? She was the reincarnation of Xander's lost love, whether she'd asked to be or not. Her wolf was mated to his now, whether she'd asked for it or not. And all this time, he'd been —

He'd been a perfect gentleman, ever since the night of the full moon. More than that — he'd been her wisecracking English knight in tarnished armor. Rushing to her rescue. Trying to hold her broken pieces together even when she could feel through the link that doing so was cracking his brittle facade into smaller and smaller shards.

He'd opened his home to her. Opened a vein for her. And the wolf inside her needed to get to him *right now*, like she needed her next breath.

Still weeping softly, Manisha untied her robe and let it fall, dropping to all fours beside the pile of thick terrycloth as her body twisted and changed. With a surge of relief, she rushed forward to lick and nuzzle at her mate's jaw, even as she whimpered her distress over the loss of Sangye and her fear about the future.

Her mate slung a front paw over her shoulder and lapped at her cheek with slow, reassuring strokes. Manisha flopped down, tangling their bodies together, and rolled onto her side. A feeling of safety and protection flooded her as Xander curled himself around her, still licking her fur with the same soothing rhythm. She pressed her body more fully against his comforting warmth, letting her human grief and worry float away into the ether.

He'd been right. The wolf lived only in the moment. Manisha was warm. Her belly was full.

The male with whom she'd bonded was next to her, keeping watch against the night. Everything else could wait until she was rested. Her eyes slipped closed, the human bedroom replaced by visions of open fields at night, full of interesting smells and the scampering of small prey animals.

Manisha slept, her legs twitching with small movements as she dreamed of running side by side with her mate—the sky a wide, black expanse above them, shot through with stars.

NINETEEN

It was still dark when a hand stroked over her skull and down her spine, waking her. Even though he was in his human form now, the wolf still recognized her mate. She yawned in contentment, jaw cracking. Muscles pulled deliciously beneath her skin as she indulged in a slow, full-body stretch.

"Manisha," he said, "*Christ*. I've just realized something. It's important. We need to talk to the others again."

The fuzzy cloth covering she'd worn earlier in human form reappeared, draping across her body.

"Come back to me now," he said, and shook his head. "Good god. I can't believe we've all been such idiots."

The manic edge beneath his words was enough to rouse her human sensibilities, and the wolf reluctantly stepped aside. Her body rippled and changed, leaving Manisha sprawled inelegantly on the floor at the foot of Xander's bed where the wolf had fallen asleep.

"What's wrong?" she mumbled, feeling dull and befuddled.

He helped her wrap the robe around herself properly. "Many, many things," he said, frowning. "But I realized a few minutes ago that we've all been shown up by a six-year-old. Well, a six-year-old and a terrifying old scarecrow who I always thought was one slip away from becoming humanity's second-worst nightmare."

She blinked at him, trying to bring her brain back online. "Look—I'm sorry, but I have absolutely no idea what you're trying to say."

His mouth ticked up as though he were attempting to smile, but his brows were still drawn together in a frown. "That's because you already said it. Not your fault that the rest of us weren't paying attention. Neither Snag nor Sangye ever drank human blood, except for the initial bloodlust where they had no control."

She still wasn't getting it, but she let him help her to her feet and lead her out by the hand.

"I've summoned the others," he was saying. "They should be trying to get Oksana, Mason, and Duchess back on the line, though it'll be daytime in Singapore so they may be asleep."

"Um… okay?" she said, following him back to the living area, where the others were also trailing in with varying expressions of curiosity and grogginess.

"What's up?" Della asked, pushing her sleep-tangled hair back from her face. She flopped down on the nearest sofa and raised an eyebrow at Xander's obvious agitation.

"Let the others get here first," Xander said, urging Manisha to join her on the couch and turning to pace restlessly around the room.

Eris and Trynn arrived next. Manisha couldn't help noticing that Eris looked like death warmed over—pale and exhausted, with dark circles under his eyes. Trynn wasn't faring much better.

Finally, Tré crossed the room to place the laptop in front of them. The blonde woman, Duchess, was alone on the screen this time.

"Where are Mason and Oksana?" Xander asked.

"Sleeping," Duchess said, looking perfectly put together right down to her blood-red lipstick. "I didn't want to wake them until I knew what was happening."

"Get them," Xander insisted. "Everyone needs to hear this."

She lifted a sculpted brow, and tilted her head, her eyes going distant for a moment. "Very well. They're on their way, *mon chou*. While we're waiting, please take a deep breath. You're making me twitchy, and I'm half a world away."

Xander stopped pacing, but the tension in his spine did not subside. After a brief wait, the Australian doctor and the sweet-faced black woman, Oksana, came into camera range and sat down, obviously freshly awoken.

"What's wrong?" Oksana asked.

Xander sat down next to Manisha, his knee jiggling restlessly. "We're all fools, that's what's wrong."

There was a beat of silence, before Trynn said, "A little clarification here, maybe?"

Xander sucked in a breath and let it flow out, as if trying to marshal his words. "We've been fighting this battle against Bael, but we've been throwing him boxes full of ammunition to use against us at the same time." He ran a hand through his hair in frustration. "A *six-year-old* figured this out, for Christ's sake—and we didn't. Snag figured it out millennia ago, and if we find him in one piece I'm going to kick his bony arse for not spelling it out to the rest of us."

"Xander…" Tré said.

Xander shot to his feet again, too wired to stay still. "Right—sorry. It's so *obvious*, though. *You can't fight evil when you're stealing people's blood and preying on them.* You can't be the good guys under those circumstances, not even when you're stealing their blood from them very nicely and politely. Don't you see? We're part of the very darkness we're trying to fight!"

Manisha blinked, finally understanding what he was getting at. She knew, though, that she didn't have enough of a view into their world to truly offer an opinion. Which wasn't true for the others, clearly.

"Oh, my god," Oksana said softly.

"Too long without drinking blood," Tré said, "and we won't be fighting anyone or anything, Xander. You know that."

Xander shook his head in frustration. "Listen, though. Della. Trynn. Mason. Have any of you drunk blood from innocents yet?"

"No," Della said. "I just… haven't been able to face that, yet."

"No," Trynn echoed. "Only from Eris. Oh—and once from Oksana, when I got hurt in Damascus."

There was a short pause. "Yes. I... drank from my brother," said Mason.

Xander cocked an eyebrow. "Did he offer first?"

"Well, of course," Mason said. "I would hardly have done it otherwise."

"Good," said Xander. "That's good."

Tré frowned at him. "Is it? *Tovarăş,* our mates can only indulge in their preference not to hunt if some of us feed from humans. And when we are feeding another vampire, we must hunt more often than if we were only providing for ourselves. The same thing goes for Snag. Eris is providing for both him and Trynn." His pale eyes met Manisha's for a moment before moving back to Xander. "And as to the boy, if he has been starving himself, he will eventually become too weak to function. I'm afraid I fail to understand the point you're making."

Trynn looked uncertain. "I mean... I suppose we could try stealing from blood banks instead of hunting, but..."

Della shook her head. "But that's even worse. Being drained by a vampire doesn't do any lasting harm to a person. But the blood supply is always tight, and when someone needs a transfusion, it's usually life threatening. We'd be stealing from those in real need."

"No." The voice came from the laptop speakers—Oksana. "That's not what he means, is it, Xander?"

Xander mustered a faint twitch of a smile for her. "Score one for the snack food addict," he said, relief coloring his tone. "Now, please tell me I'm not crazy."

Duchess snorted.

"No comment," said Oksana, "but I won't hold it against you in this case. It's a frighteningly valid point."

Mason raised his eyebrows. "You're thinking about the girls in Haiti, aren't you?"

Xander nodded. "Yes. The girls in Haiti. And your brother."

Oksana nodded as well.

"What girls in Haiti?" Della asked in confusion.

Oksana smiled. "When we were preparing to rescue the children, the mambo we were staying with brought in some volunteers from the village. Haitians are more aware of the supernatural—and more comfortable with it—than many cultures. The three girls who came knew what we were and offered their blood freely."

"Their siblings were among the kidnapping victims," Mason added. "They wanted to help get them back in whatever way they could."

Tré looked between them. "So, you're proposing... what?"

"I'm proposing that we stop doing evil things when we're supposed to be fighting evil," Xander said.

Manisha spoke up. "Do you think you can find other people who would willingly offer blood? I mean, do you have friends who know about you being vampires, or—?"

"No," Eris said flatly. "We don't."

"Yes," Mason contradicted, "we do. Maybe not many. But I already told you that my brother Jackson knows. His wife does, too, though she's understandably still a bit wary of us. And a colleague of mine, Dr. Belawen."

"There are several people in Haiti," Oksana added. "Mama Lovelie, the girls we already talked about, and a retired healer in the same village."

"Madame Francine, in New Orleans," Della added.

"And a former employee of hers named Madeleine," Xander mused. "Though she may well be a werewolf by now."

Manisha looked at him sharply.

"Voluntarily," he was quick to add. "The man she was in love with became a werewolf, and she followed him."

She couldn't imagine anyone signing up for such a thing voluntarily, but she let it go.

"As interesting as this is," Duchess said, "pursuing it would be a logistical nightmare."

"It's hardly our biggest concern right now," Eris said tightly.

There was a beat, and then Della said, "Well, I think it's a good idea." The words were quiet, and she didn't look at the rest of them, her eyes fixed firmly on her hands lying folded in her lap.

"I agree," Oksana put in immediately.

Several of the others were looking at Tré, who seemed to be the de facto leader of the group. Tré, in turn, was looking at Xander.

"You have more to say on this matter, I think," he said, holding Xander's gaze steadily. "So, *tovarăş* — convince me."

-o-o-o-

Xander met his best friend's disconcerting pale gaze, and tried not to think about what he was poised to reveal. There were things about him that none of them knew; things that the selfish part of him would much rather keep hidden in the dark. But he'd had an epiphany earlier tonight — one that the others hadn't caught up with yet, it was clear.

He didn't let his gaze waver as he said, "I think I finally understand the true nature of the war in which we're embroiled, Tré. And it's not the war we thought we'd signed up for."

Tré nodded slowly. "Very well. Explain that to us."

He tore his eyes away and ran a hand through his hair, agitated. Unable to keep still, he started to pace again, a few steps in one direction, a few steps in the other, trying not to think about the bottles of spiked blood in the hidden refrigerator, only a room away.

"Right. So. We've been looking at this as a fight. A battle where Bael throws things at us and we fight them off. Bombs. Riots. Undead soldiers. He attacks and we counter. Sometimes we think we've won, sometimes we know we've lost, and along the way we pick up more soldiers, hoping that if we can get the magic number thirteen, it will somehow change the rules of the game."

"The prophecy about the Council of Thirteen is the only hope of victory we've been able to find," Eris grated, sounding like he was nearing the end of his tether.

Xander's jaw clenched, but he forced himself not to rise to the bait. Not to let things devolve into sniping and avoidance the way he normally would.

"Yes," he said. "But, Eris, it's a battle between Light and Darkness. If we're supposed to be on the side of Light, why are we fighting with guns and knives and claws and fangs? Why are we allowing the Darkness to dictate the terms of the battle?"

He paused to let the words sink in.

Duchess' voice emerged from the laptop speakers. "Xander. We are vampires. We are all dark creatures. Darkness is woven into our very natures."

And that was the perfect segue into the thing he didn't want to talk about. The desire for a few pints of blood containing something in the illegal opioid or narcotic family grew stronger, making his palms itch.

"It is," he agreed. "For some of us, it's woven more deeply than others. But we have true innocents among our numbers now, as well. A child of six? A pediatric doctor who volunteers in fucking *war zones*? A trio of women whose only crime was trying to live their lives, hurting no one?"

Xander looked at Tré again—a man as close to him as a brother. Noble to a fault, but not a saint. Not after six centuries walking the Earth. He looked at Duchess—the ice queen who had spent hundreds of years punishing herself for a crime she'd never shared with any of them. At Eris, the professional art thief and tomb raider. Oksana, who had ripped her own leg off and dug free of the grave she'd been buried in, savaging an innocent teenager who'd been left there to keep watch.

"One day soon," he said, "the nature of this war is going to change, and all of our darkness is going to be dragged forward into the light. Don't you get it? It's *spiritual warfare*. And I choose, right here and now, to pull my darkness into the light on my own terms."

Xander realized, with a faint feeling of shock, that his hands were physically trembling. He tucked them under his arms and kept pacing. His goddamned shields were wavering, too. He could feel Manisha's curiosity and concern brushing up against his senses.

Then Tré's grounding mental voice. *We already know each other's darkness, old friend. There is no need to dwell on it, surely.*

But he shook his head, speaking aloud since his friends in Singapore were too far away for him to link with them mentally. "No. There are things about me none of you know. Things that will change the way you view me, and rightfully so. I don't know if those things can ever be balanced out, but I have been a parasite since long before I ever became a bloodsucker. And that, at least, is going to have to change. Starting today."

He heard Manisha draw in a breath and recognized that he'd been wrong earlier—there was one person here who already knew about the sins of his past. The sharp stab of pain he felt in response to that realization was irrational. She would have remembered sooner or later what sort of creature her wolf had bonded to, and he might as well face her disgust at the same time he faced all of the others'.

He wondered if any of them would still call him friend an hour from now. Duchess, maybe, he thought. Or perhaps not, given her soft spot for children. Eris, he was even less sure of—they barely tolerated each other at the best of times. And if he thought too closely about either Tré or Oksana turning their backs on him, he'd talk himself right out of this bloody madness before he even started.

Oddly, he found himself wishing Snag were here. Snag had seen some shit. There probably wasn't much *anyone* could come up with that would shock Snag.

Tell them. It was Manisha's voice. *I think you're right about this war.*

He swallowed and closed his eyes.

TWENTY

Manisha realized what Xander was working up to all at once, dream images bubbling up in her mind from the distant past. *Oh.* No wonder he was upset.

The reality of what it meant to be on the front lines of a war between good and evil suddenly pulled into sharp focus before her eyes. It was no surprise that none of the others had looked at it in such a way before. It simply wasn't human nature — or vampire nature, she suspected — to react to a blatantly physical attack by asking how one could become a better person. No, it was human — or vampire — nature to defend against the attack and fight back in kind.

Tell them, she urged Xander silently, convinced in this moment that he had discovered an important key to what was happening around them. *I think you're right about this war.*

She could feel his tightly controlled distress over what he assumed her reaction would be. Her reaction, and the others'. But he wasn't taking into account that she had been a part of his secret shame, too. Perhaps not as she was today — as Manisha — but that long-ago lifetime as Eliza was still part of her karma. She would be a hypocrite if she condemned Xander without also condemning herself.

And if his friends condemned him? She could feel her wolf bristle, ready to defend its mate against any threat—even if that threat came from those he thought of as family. Manisha couldn't control the others' reactions, but she could ensure that Xander didn't face them alone.

She saw his throat bob and his eyes slip closed. A moment later, he began to speak in a flat, faraway tone.

"You're all content to hand matters of finance over to me," he said. "To let me be the one to worry about making enough money to provide what we need, so we can travel at a moment's notice... live wherever we need to live... surround ourselves with comfort when we're not busy fighting for our lives." He gestured around the extravagant penthouse flat.

Tré cocked his head. "You have a talent for business, Xander. You always have. It only makes sense to utilize it."

"A talent for business," Xander echoed softly. "A talent gained by pulling myself out of the gutter a farthing at a time, beginning when I was thirteen years old—the youngest son of a struggling coal merchant. Ten years later, I was one of the richest men in London. Tell me... do you think I managed that feat without climbing over the broken bodies of those less ruthless than I was?"

There was a beat of silence before Eris said, "We've all done things we're not proud of, Xander. What's your point?"

"When I was thirteen, I stole half of my mother's savings—a handful of pennies—and used it to buy waste cotton from a local mill. Anything with defects that I could get my hands on, I sold at a profit to private seamstresses who couldn't afford first-quality bolts. By the time I was fifteen, I had standing contracts with a dozen mills to take their seconds and overages at a discounted price.

"When I was eighteen, I started brokering deals with orphanages. I arranged for them to *apprentice* any children between the ages of eleven and fourteen to the cotton mills in exchange for a percentage of the wage savings the owners enjoyed as a result. When I was twenty, I talked a doddering old banker into giving me a loan and bought my first mill."

The room was perfectly still. Manisha closed her eyes, reliving hazy half-memories of touring the newly completed bunkhouses next to the textile factory where the orphans—the so-called apprentices—slept in shifts when they weren't working.

"I worked those children twelve hours a day, six days a week, and the adult employees fourteen hours a day. I paid the orphans three shillings a week, and the orphanage took half of that. My overseers sent the smallest children to crawl inside the machinery for cleaning and repair. The conditions were horrible. Within three years, I'd purchased nine more mills, thanks to my knack for keeping labor costs so low and productivity so high.

"Meanwhile, I lived in a stylish mansion with Eliza and a bevy of servants, surrounded by luxury. A parasite living off the sweat and labor of children, spending my days finding new loopholes in the pathetic excuses for labor laws that were all they had to protect them."

Movement on the laptop screen drew Manisha's eye. Duchess rose silently and disappeared from the camera's view. Manisha felt a sharp ache cut through Xander's chest as she left without a word, but he continued to speak.

"I lived that life of ease right up until the night a demon decided that either my money or my ruthlessness might be valuable to him. Bael recognized my blighted soul for exactly what it was, and turned me into a leech of the far more literal variety. If thinking about it in those terms didn't make me want to stake myself, it would probably be fucking hilarious."

He turned away abruptly and walked into the kitchen. A moment later, he crossed to the hallway leading back to the bedrooms, pausing with his hand on the wall. The other held a glass bottle, its contents the deepest crimson.

"So," he said, not looking back at them, "if you want to know why I, at least, need to stop being a literal parasite on humanity... that's why. Now, I just have to figure out if I know any humans who give enough of a shit about me to open a vein for this particular cut-rate Count Dracula."

With that, he disappeared into the back of the flat, leaving a heavy pall of silence behind him.

"Shit," Mason said, his voice sounding flat and shocked over the computer's speakers.

There was another long stretch of nothing. Manisha let more of the hazy images from the past slide across her mind, thinking back to those days spent in a world a hundred years before she'd been born.

"Tré..." Oksana's soft voice emerged from the screen.

The silver-eyed leader roused himself from his introspection. "Yes," he said. "I'm going, Oksana." He looked around, meeting each of their eyes in turn. "It was a different time. In many ways, that does not excuse it. But childhood was not the same in the past as it is today. In my village, boys and girls as young as four worked the fields from dawn until dusk, and no one would ever have thought to question it. It simply... *was*."

Eris nodded. "Yes. The past was... a different world. A grimmer world. As children, we either worked, or our families starved."

Tré rose and headed after Xander. Manisha quickly scrambled up to follow him, meeting his eyes with a challenging gaze. "I'm going with you."

He assessed her for a beat before speaking. "And what will you say to him? Whether you realize it or not, Manisha, you hold the sharpened stake he talked about in your hand right now."

She narrowed her eyes at him, the wolf rumbling a warning at him in her mind. "Unlike the rest of you, I was there with him—living in that beautiful mansion. So, I'll take whatever portion of blame my spirit deserves, and then I'll remind him of some of the things he so carefully left out while he was so busy painting himself in the worst possible light."

Tré lifted his chin, regarding her, and then nodded his approval. "Very well. Come on, then."

-o-o-o-

They found Xander in the master bedroom, sprawled in a high-backed chair. He was holding the bottle in one hand, turning it slowly back and forth, staring at the facets in the crimson liquid as though he might find the secrets of the universe reflected therein. He did not look up as they entered.

Manisha marched over and took the bottle from him, setting it on the low table next to his chair. He looked up at her warily, his eyes flicking over her shoulder to Tré, and then back to focus on a point near her chin — not meeting her gaze.

Not really thinking before she moved, she darted a hand out and twisted it in his neatly pressed collar, pulling him forward and bending down until their lips met. He froze in surprise, and she shivered minutely at the frisson as their skin touched — so different now than the sharp, shocking jolt she'd felt when his hand had first brushed hers in the warehouse stairwell.

He made a noise into the kiss, quiet and startled. For a moment, he melted into her — only to catch himself, stiffening and pulling away carefully. Cautious green eyes lifted to meet hers.

"Why?" he asked, the word emerging chary and guarded.

She could feel him in her mind… feel that cold, reflective surface that meant he was shielding his thoughts from her. The smooth mirror was rippling now, though, struck glass resonating like a tuning fork. Manisha loosened her grip on his shirt and placed her hand on the center of his chest, palm flat. Following some newly awakened instinct, she did the same thing mentally, pressing her thoughts against the glass barrier he held between them.

The mirror shattered, brilliant shards raining down.

Beyond, she felt the buzz of conflicted emotions, the itch of an addict resisting the siren lure of self-medication, the pain of someone who had never and would never extend to himself the same forgiveness and leniency he offered those he cared about. She also felt the echo of his bonds with the others — most notably, the man in the room with them now.

We are still here, tovarăș, Tré said, his mental voice every bit as deep and reassuring as his physical one. *Do you think you mean so little to us that the sins of your past would make a difference in our regard for you?*

Manisha let her fingertips slide away from his chest as Xander curled forward in the chair, ducking his face. His hand covered his eyes for a moment, and it was shaking. Then he scrubbed at his forehead and straightened. He looked... fragile. Every bit as much in danger of shattering as his mental barriers had been.

"If I'm right about this war," he said hoarsely, "I may be a liability you'd do better without, Tré. Even if Duchess decides to forgive me for what I did when I was human, there may not be enough lipstick in the world to dress up this particular swine in time for the party."

"You're talking drivel," Manisha snapped, and pressed hazy images into his mind.

Alexander Grimshaw, paying doctors out of his own pocket to treat his employees when they were sick or injured… slipping his workers money off the books to deal with family emergencies… stocking the orphans' lodgings with books and toys… hiring tutors to school them on their days off.

Tré huffed in the background. *Of course. Why am I not surprised in the least?* he sent through the bond.

Xander surged to his feet, as if he couldn't bear to sit still while those memories slipped into his mind.

"Tiny dribs and drabs of benevolence to act as a balm for my pricking conscience," he snarled. "Meaningless tokens!"

She blocked his path before he could start pacing again. *"Meaningless?* I doubt they were meaningless to the people receiving them!"

"Oh? Do you know what would make that argument valid?" he shot back, biting off the words. "What would make that argument valid was if I had kept only as much money to live on as I paid to the lowest of my employees. Had I done that, and reinvested everything else in the people who worked and toiled and slaved for me, those mills might not have been the hellholes that they were. *But I didn't."*

"But *we* didn't, you mean," Manisha said. "You weren't the only one to benefit from the money made by those mills."

He waved off the words. "You're *not Eliza.* Manisha, you have never at any point in your life had the slightest control of or influence over what happened more than a century ago. Hell, given the social mores of the time, Eliza didn't have a whole lot of influence over it, either."

"You think so?" Manisha asked. "Because I distinctly remember being asked if I wanted to own a beautiful London mansion, and I remember how simple it was to justify answering 'yes' to myself."

"*Enough,* you two." Tré's words cut through the standoff, dragging both of their attention to him. "None of this can be changed. Everyone who ever worked for you back then is dead, Xander. Most of them have been dead for a very long time. You were a human being who did both good and evil in the world. So were we all."

Xander fell back into the chair again. "Fuck you, Tré. You're so goddamned noble it makes me want to puke. You always have been."

Tré seemed unperturbed by the casual abuse, only raising an eyebrow. "Hardly. I was raised the privileged child of a nobleman, taught from the time I could crawl that I had more worth than the people around me. A lesson I absorbed wholeheartedly, and put into practice with everyone I knew. Had I survived to take my father's position, who knows what damage I could have done. But I didn't survive, and neither did you. We were attacked by Bael. We will never know how those lives would have turned out."

"And now you both fight to save the world from darkness, even though the darkness has already tried to claim you," Manisha added.

"Yes," Tré said. "We do."

TWENTY-ONE

The door creaked open. "Yup. That all sounds about right to me," Trynn said.

The others followed. Eris fetched up against the doorframe, his arms crossed. Della was carrying the laptop. She slipped past him into the room and set it on the neatly made bed.

Oksana was still on the Skype call, though Mason had gone.

"Xander," she said kindly.

He looked at the screen. "Oksana. Did Ozzie do a runner as well, then?"

"He went to talk to Duchess." She regarded him fondly through the camera. "You know how she gets when children are involved, *ti mwen*. She'll eventually come around, and realize what the rest of us already know."

"And what's that?" Xander asked, sounding tired.

Her voice was gentle. "That everyone makes mistakes, and everyone deserves an opportunity for redemption."

Manisha decided that she liked Xander's friends.

Trynn made herself comfortable leaning against the bed's headboard. "Hey, that reminds me. You still never told me what your current company does, Xander. What exactly is paying for all these chartered helicopters and penthouse apartments?"

A soft laugh came from the laptop.

Trynn peered around to look at the screen. "What's so funny?"

Oksana shook her head. "Ah, you'll see. Tell her, Xander."

That was enough to make Manisha curious as well.

"Photovoltaic cells, mostly," he muttered.

She got the joke at the same moment Trynn did, judging by the other woman's startled bark of laughter. "Oh my god," Trynn said. "You run a vampire-controlled *solar panel* company?"

Della's expression was priceless, and Manisha suspected hers was as well.

"We're branching out into wind turbine technology, too," Xander said under his breath.

"Perhaps now you'll finally be able to inspect your products while they're in use," Tré suggested. "Without succumbing to horrific burn injuries in the process, I mean."

Eris made a frustrated sound. "As heartwarming as all of this is, we have other things to worry about right now. The rest of this is just a distraction."

Manisha turned to look at him, and so did the others. His arms were crossed tightly; his body language tense. He really did look awful, and she wondered if he'd spent the hours since they first retired trying to mentally contact this ancient vampire friend of his who'd surrendered himself to their enemy. They stared at him, and he stared back, frustration and more than a hint of anger behind his gold-flecked brown gaze.

"I keep asking myself why the rest of you aren't more focused on what really matters, here," he said.

"We are focused on several things that matter, Eris," Tré said mildly. "Chief among those, the fact that we have no actionable leads, and that we are in need of a few hours, at least, to recuperate from injuries and exhaustion."

"Have you truly not made the connection?" Eris pushed away from the wall and uncrossed his arms. "This child—Sangye—*does not have a mate.*"

"What are you talking about?" Manisha asked, Eris' combative manner still rubbing her wolf the wrong way. "He's six years old!"

"And you said his mother sacrificed herself for him?" Eris asked.

It took a moment to work out what he meant, but she remembered them saying that it was the willing sacrifice of a loved one that made a vampire, earlier when they'd been talking about Sangye's refusal to drink human blood.

"Yes, that's right," she said warily. "At least, I think that's what must have happened."

Eris looked at the others again, a furrow between his brows. "Don't you *see*? Sangye killed his mother only a short time ago. Even if her spirit were to be immediately reincarnated, she wouldn't be born for months."

"Oh," Xander said blankly. "*Oh.* Son of a *bitch.*"

"Yes. Things are clearly coming to a head. Look around. There are nine of us." Eris gestured around the room, the movement encompassing the laptop and the vampires on the other end of the Skype call. "Add in Duchess' mate. Snag. Snag's mate. That's twelve. And an unattached boy with no spiritual connection to a living person—"

"Makes thirteen." Xander ran a hand through his hair. "Bloody hell."

Manisha looked between them, noting that the others looked a bit shell-shocked, too. "You said something earlier about the number thirteen. Something about a... prophecy?"

"The Council of Thirteen," Della said quietly. "It's supposedly the only thing that can stand against Bael's darkness."

"There were six original vampires," Tré explained. "Those of us who were turned by Bael over the course of several millennia. For a long time, we assumed that there were other vampires and we simply had not found them... or perhaps they had once existed but had been destroyed."

Della took up the thread again. "This prophecy pops up in a few different places, but the gist is that the Council will be made up of thirteen of Bael's greatest failures and that once it comes together, it will be able to fight him."

A small shock went through her as she did the math. "Wait. So you think *I'm* part of this somehow?" She shook her head, trying to clear it. "And... what's that part about 'greatest failures'?"

"You are Xander's mate," Tré said, not unkindly. "The reincarnation of the soul who saved him through a willing sacrifice."

Her eyes flew to Xander, but he was looking down and would not meet her gaze.

"As for the failure part," Trynn said. "Bael was originally trying to turn our mates into puppets—creatures like Bastian Kovac who would exist only to do his bidding." Her voice went rough with hatred on the name, and Manisha's wolf growled in solidarity. "But Bael discounted the power of love. Instead of mindless servants, he ended up with vampires who hate him with every fiber of their beings. Who will stop at nothing to see him destroyed."

Della's hazel eyes snapped. "And it's not just the original vampires. We are also his failures. He thought we were dead. He discounted us. But death wasn't enough to keep our souls apart from the ones we love. We came back, and we found those we'd lost."

Her words made something in Manisha's chest ache for a moment before it settled into place and eased. There was a terrible and beautiful sort of symmetry to what she had just been told.

Eris met her eyes and spoke. "Bael tried to remove you from the chessboard by making you into a werewolf—bait for Xander that he could chase, but never truly possess. Yet even in that, he failed. After all these countless years, he still has no conception of the true power of love. It is foreign to him—impenetrable and unknowable."

The feeling of possessive satisfaction she felt upon hearing those words was pure wolf. When she turned glowing eyes back to Xander, it was to find him looking up at her with an expression of painful hope and longing on his haggard features. As their eyes met, though, he tore his gaze free and looked away again.

"I dragged you into this by virtue of my very existence—and for that, I'm sorry," he said. "None of us asked for this, but I don't think that there's any way for us to escape it now."

"I don't want to escape it," she said. "I want to find Sangye and this other vampire friend of yours. And then I want us to stop this creature who delights in spreading pain and darkness across the world."

This time, their eyes locked and held. Green light flared behind Xander's gaze.

"Good," Tré said from behind her. "Now, we just need to decide our next step. Eris? I assume you and Trynn attempted to reach Snag again? Did you have any success?"

With difficulty, Manisha dragged her attention away from Xander and back to the conversation.

Eris shook his head in frustration. "There's nothing. No trace, no sense of his existence."

"Which merely means that he is not nearby, correct?" Tré asked. "Not that he is necessarily dead."

"Yes, that's correct."

Oksana spoke. "I still think that Xander is onto something. Perhaps we should all meet somewhere that we can find humans willing to feed us voluntarily. Which, right now, probably means either here in Singapore, or back in Haiti."

Mason and Duchess reappeared in camera range and rejoined her. The blonde woman appeared pale, but composed.

"I disagree on the subject of devoting large amounts of effort toward finding volunteers to feed us," Duchess said evenly. "If the option is readily available, that's fine. Otherwise, it puts us at too much of a tactical disadvantage."

"I agree." That was Eris. "I don't have time to devote to wild theories when Snag and the boy are in Bael's hands. I also have no intention of jetting halfway around the world when the most logical place to start a search is near the area where they went missing."

Tré lifted his chin and drew everyone in with his gaze. "Very well. Both arguments have merit. Xander, if those of us who are already here were to start searching outward from the UK and into Western Europe, would there be any option for those who wish to stop hunting and only drink blood that is freely given?"

Xander looked utterly exhausted, but he drew his shoulders back and nodded. "Possibly. I'll start trying to find employees inside HelioTeque who can be trusted with the truth." He scrubbed a hand across his eyes. "One thing about it—if they lose their shit when they find out their boss is a vampire, I can always mesmerize them into forgetting it again."

"Mind-whammy to the rescue," Trynn muttered.

Manisha wondered with a jolt if her new thirst for blood meant she would also be able to influence humans' minds, as she'd seen Sangye do to the hapless teenagers Crank had dragged in for him to feed on. She blinked free of the startling thought and focused on the matter at hand.

"I have relatives in Swansea," she said in a hesitant voice. "They're not particularly close—second and third cousins, mostly—but they do at least know who I am. It's conceivable that if I told them what happened with Sangye, they'd help. Of course, it's also conceivable they'd run screaming in the other direction." She shrugged.

"It's worth a try," Tré said. "Those of us who are already here will start our search outward from London. Duchess… Oksana… Mason… do you intend to join us?"

Duchess shook her head. "Not immediately. There are reports coming out of Malaysia that are… unsettling. Singapore is a good base of operations from which to monitor things for a few more weeks."

"But do contact us right away if you learn anything new about Snag or Sangye, obviously," Oksana added. "Travel in this area is relatively undisrupted—so far, at least, and we can get to you pretty fast if we need to."

"In that case," Tré said, "is everyone agreed on this general course of action?"

There were shrugs and expressions of agreement, including a tight nod from Eris, who still looked deeply unhappy. Tré's silver gaze played over Xander for a moment before coming to rest on Manisha.

Do you two wish some time alone? The words whispered quietly inside her mind.

She recognized the leader's mental voice, and got the impression that the question had only been for her and Xander to hear.

Xander's brow furrowed. *I'm not sure that's a good —*

Yes, she thought as clearly and loudly as she could, cutting him off—only to flush when Eris, Trynn, and Della snapped around to look at her. *Whoops.*

"Don't feel bad," Trynn said. "I nearly shouted Eris' ear off when I was trying to learn that trick. But, yeah, when you project that loudly we can all hear it. So… yes to what, exactly?"

"Yes, it would be best if the rest of us returned to our hotel before dawn, and left these two in peace," Tré answered, saving Manisha the added embarrassment. "There is still time if we leave now, and we can reconvene here tonight, once we've all had a chance to rest properly."

The tense line of Xander's shoulders eased. "Take some of the bottled blood with you, if you want. I won't be getting more using the methods I have in the past, but since it's already here, there's no further ethical stain involved in drinking it. Pouring it down the drain would only make it a waste on top of everything else."

"No argument here. Dibs on one of the spiked bottles," Trynn said tiredly.

"We'll leave you lot to it, then," Mason said from the laptop. "Keep us posted. And Xander? Chin up, mate. You may be an arsehole, but you're still *our* arsehole."

"I'm choking up over here, Ozzie," Xander said.

After a brief round of farewells, the Singapore contingent signed off. A few moments later the others were gathering bottles from the fridge and heading out. Della paused and wrapped Manisha in a brief, one-armed hug. Caught by surprise, she hugged back, realizing with a pang how long it had been since she'd had any female friends who just... did things like that.

My pack, the wolf insisted.

Her eyes squeezed shut as Della murmured, "Hang in there, okay? The world sucks... but you two still found each other despite the odds. Grab onto the good things and hold tight. Don't let go."

"Thanks," Manisha whispered.

Trynn gave her a pat on the shoulder and a sympathetic smile as well, and then the pair of women returned to Tré and Eris' sides. Tré gave Manisha a solemn nod, and even Eris dipped his chin in farewell before the group disappeared through the door. The flat seemed very quiet once their footsteps had faded into silence.

TWENTY-TWO

"You never answered my question, you know," Xander said quietly, once they were alone.

Manisha blinked at him, hoping it was only the combination of exhaustion and mental overload that was making her feel stupid. "What question is that?" she asked.

Rather than answer, he walked into the kitchen and returned a moment later with a bottle, which he pressed into her hands. "Here, drink this. The mental confusion and that gnawing feeling you're trying to ignore means the cravings are about to return. You should learn to recognize when your body needs blood." He made an awkward gesture toward the bottle. "Don't worry. This is the un-spiked stuff."

Her mouth started to water, and she swallowed hard. "*What question?*" she repeated, trying to focus on him and not the draw of the red liquid in her hand.

His lips pressed together, and he replied, "Drink that first, and then I'll tell you."

She unscrewed the cap, and as soon as the smell hit her nostrils, her fangs lengthened, poking the insides of her cheeks. Her stomach cramped. She lifted the bottle to her lips cautiously. The first drop touched her tongue, and her vision went blurry. When she came back to herself, the bottle was empty and she was licking around the opening, trying to get her tongue inside as low growling noises emerged from her throat.

Shocked, she jerked her head back and let the glass container drop as though it had suddenly become red hot. A hand darted out to catch it neatly before it could shatter on the pristine tile floor.

"Shit!" she gasped, staggering back a couple of steps. "What did I just—?"

"The first few days can be a bit overwhelming. Try not to worry about it. In a pinch, you can always drink from me if there isn't a bottle to hand."

He wasn't looking at her, instead pretending to examine the bottle's label. She could only imagine what she'd looked like—an animal trying to lick up every last drop of gore—snarling over its prize. Humiliation flooded her, growing even deeper when she remembered that there was a very good chance the man standing in front of her could hear every thought running through her head. He must think she was pathetic... must be wondering why he'd ever let this pitiful, out-of-control freak of nature through his doors—

"No, Manisha." The words, spoken aloud, broke through her litany of self-recrimination. "That's... really not the direction my thoughts were taking..."

She looked at him, still mute, and he huffed out a sharp breath.

"Sorry," he said. "I'd assumed you'd figured it out by now. You drew the short straw and ended up with the perverted vampire. I'd apologize for it again, but I'm afraid it's pretty much hard-wired in at this point."

Manisha stared, trying to decide if he was being honest or just trying to make her feel better. Belatedly, it occurred to her to look inward, through the link—which she did, just in time to detect a flash of discomfort from him.

"I could, er, probably call Tré and Della back if you'd be more comfortable staying with them..." he said.

With difficulty, she shook off her embarrassment over her lapse of control.

"Why? Are you trying to get rid of me?" she asked.

I'm trying to protect you, you stubborn woman. Something about the faint air of desperation lurking under the words made her think he hadn't intended her to hear them. This was confirmed a moment later, when he said, "I'm trying to do the right thing, that's all. Several people over the years have intimated that I should try it sometime. This seemed like the perfect opportunity."

"You still haven't told me what question I didn't answer," she reminded him.

He turned and set the bottle carefully on the bar that separated the kitchen from the living area. "You kissed me. Afterward, I asked you why, and you didn't answer."

Surprise threaded through her. *I did an awful lot more than kiss you when we were trapped in the freezer, and you barely batted an eyelash,* she thought.

He glanced at her sideways. "You were out of your head at the time," he said, "and you didn't know me from Adam."

"My wolf knew you," she said.

"*You* didn't know what sort of... person I was. But now you do. And you still kissed me again."

"My wolf knows you, even now."

The growing intensity of his green gaze made something jump, low in her stomach. Inside her, the wolf stretched and pricked its ears.

"Why are you still here, Manisha?" he asked, tone vehement... as though the answer were vitally important to him. *Why haven't you run away from me yet?* echoed silently in the background.

Behind her stretched the crumbled bridge of her life, its broken pieces toppled into a bottomless ravine, irretrievable. Ahead of her stood a man with hand outstretched, offering her a strong arm to pull her onto the stony ledge of the future. Others might have seen a monster. They might have seen a cold, sharp-witted bastard.

Her wolf saw its mate. And Manisha—

She saw the man who had come for her when she was in danger. Who had held her in his arms like a cracked treasure, gluing her broken pieces together and propping her up until she was strong enough to stand on her own again. Who had done all those things while harboring the utter certainty that she would flee in horror the moment she remembered their shared past; her life—and death—as his beloved Eliza.

"I'm here because our souls are connected," she said, the truth of the words weaving around her like a spell even as she spoke them. "I'm here because we belong together."

An instant later, her face was cradled in Xander's hands, and he was kissing her like he wanted to drink her down... as though her breath was the finest wine. In the back of her mind, she heard a desperate whisper. *Please, please, please, for the love of god, don't let me wake up from this and find it was only a drug-fueled hallucination.*

Something about that mental whisper nearly shattered her heart, and she wrapped herself around him, deepening the kiss. The wolf inside her rumbled in satisfaction at the rightness of the feeling. She realized distantly that the low, animal noise was actually vibrating up from her chest, and decided she didn't care. If he hadn't been put off by her practically tongue-fucking a wine bottle to get at the dregs of blood inside, she figured he could probably handle her growling at him.

Manisha, love, he thought very clearly and distinctly, pressing their bodies together until she could feel his hard length pressing into the crease of her hip, *you really have no idea.*

She stopped fighting and let the wolf lead, pulling away from his lips in favor of trailing biting kisses and licks along his strong jaw line. His hands slipped from her cheeks to her hair, and he buried his fingers in the thick mass. Shivers of lightning trailed across her scalp and down her spine, a combination of the strange spark running between them and the intimacy of the touch.

He nuzzled her cheek as she ran her lips over his face and neck. The absolute *rightness* of this feeling washed through her like a warm tide. Everything else in her life right now was wrong, frightening, and painful. The eightfold path of her religious upbringing seemed like a distant mirage, unreachable—retreating further into the distance with every step she took toward it. But here, now, with Xander's hands wrapped in her hair and his body pressing against hers from chest to knees, she could breathe, if only for a moment.

He eased her head back a few centimeters until he could rest their foreheads together. Her eyes slipped closed, her mind going blissfully blank for one precious, much-needed moment as her heated flesh pressed against his cool skin.

Just for a little while, she needed this. She needed this respite so very badly, before they once more had to face a world drowning in darkness. Maybe Xander needed it, too, because his mind was quiet even though the mirrored barrier protecting his thoughts was nowhere to be found. All she could sense was a deep, still pool of gratitude, not a ripple marring its perfect surface.

She marveled. A lifetime of daily meditation, and it was here—standing in a vampire's embrace in the short space of time between one crisis and the next—that she finally found true stillness.

"Come outside with me," he whispered into the air between them. "The sun is about to rise, and I want to watch it with you."

She nodded, a tiny movement that she knew he would feel since they were still resting forehead to forehead. "I'd like that," she murmured. How often had she wondered over the past few weeks whether she would survive to see the next sunrise?

Perhaps he heard the thought, because one of his hands dropped to encircle her shoulders and hold her tight against him. She rested there for another moment before pulling back so she could look up at him. "Come on, then. Show me London at dawn."

The large room at the end of the hall was a study, and one wall was dominated by a sliding glass door that led onto an east-facing terrace. The open space was furnished with potted plants covered in night-blooming flowers. An assortment of chairs was arranged around three sides of a small table, with a chaise lounge on the fourth side that faced out over the city. Manisha tangled her fingers with Xander's and led him to the wall at the edge of the large balcony, undeniably enchanted by their surroundings.

It was still dark out, but streaks of orange and pink painted the eastern horizon. She scanned the London cityscape, lit by millions of lights.

"Where are we?" she asked breathlessly. "Mayfair, right?"

She scanned the skyline, finding the distinctive outline of The Shard in the distance, perhaps two or three kilometers away. She craned a bit to see further to the right, where the London Eye and Big Ben could be seen much closer to them.

Xander was a solid presence behind her left shoulder. He lifted an arm, pointing almost straight ahead. "That's Trafalgar Square, with the National Gallery just a bit north of it." His finger tracked a few degrees to the left. "There's Piccadilly Circus... and just beyond that, the theater district."

She stared into the gradually lightening gray dawn for a few minutes before closing her eyes, casting her mind back to memories that both were and were not hers.

"Where was our house before?" she asked. "It was somewhere nearby, wasn't it?"

Xander was quiet for a long moment before speaking. "Yes. It was on Pall Mall."

"I'd like to see it sometime," she said, thinking of the crystal chandeliers and polished wood gleaming in firelight.

"I'm afraid it's long gone." He paused again. "There was a fire."

She let that information soak in. "That's too bad."

"Is it?" She could feel him studying her. "How can you stand to be here with me like this when you remember so much about being Eliza?" he asked eventually.

She shrugged, not sure if she would really be able to make him understand when he was so thoroughly convinced that she should be fleeing from him in horror. Tré had already tried to explain some of it, but perhaps a slightly different perspective would reach him where his friend's words had not.

"I grew up with the idea of reincarnation. It's part of the fabric of my culture and my religion. It's not a shock to me to discover that I've lived other lives. I understand the ways in which I both am and am not Eliza." She paused, choosing her words.

"Her life was tragic in many ways, but there was also joy in it. She found love. She experienced terrible poverty, but also spent time living in comfort and luxury. While it's true she turned a blind eye to the conditions in your mills, she did fight to right other social ills. And in the end, she was able to save someone she loved—even though doing so meant her death."

She heard Xander swallow before he spoke. "She should have been the one to survive. She was better than me. I should have been the one to save her, not the other way around."

Manisha turned her gaze away from the rays of weak London sunlight spilling over the edge of the horizon to look at him.

"Eliza had both light and dark in her soul, just as you did. Just as you and I still do today. Just as everyone does. But, in the same way that I am both the same person and a different person as Eliza, you are both the same man as you were then, and a different man. Now, answer me something."

"What?" His reply sounded guarded.

"How do you treat the people who work in your factories today? What are the conditions like?" She had a feeling she knew the answer, but she wanted to hear him say it.

"I... set up the largest of the production facilities in Romania, after consulting with Tré, who's from the region. Labor costs are cheaper there, so the company is able to offer generous compensation levels for the area without negatively impacting profits. There's also a research and development branch just outside London."

She nodded. "And they're well paid, too, I assume? What about the working conditions?"

"We hire an outside agency to police factory conditions and ensure that no one is tempted to cut corners as a way to inflate reporting numbers."

Manisha cocked her head at him. "So, are you going to make me say it, or can I safely assume that your intelligence is one of the things about you that *hasn't* changed?"

He was quiet for a moment. "Given the number of brain cells I've tried to destroy with illicit chemicals over the decades, I wouldn't presume to comment," he said. That fragile, hopeful look was back behind his eyes.

"Then I'll spell it out, just to be safe," she said. "You're not perfect, because *no one* is perfect. But you're also not the same man you were a hundred years ago. Now... Eliza loved that man. She died for that man. But here in the present, *you* are the one I was drawn to. Everything I've learned says that my wolf should have been drawn to my pack alpha. I should have mated Crank."

His eyes flared brilliant green, a wave of rage and denial that nearly bowled her over erupting from his end of the link. She smiled wryly.

"But I didn't," she said. "My wolf would have died before submitting to another male, because we'd already chosen *you*."

His hands closed on her upper arms as she continued to look over her shoulder at him, holding his gaze. At that moment, the morning sun reached their terrace, peeking through the gaps in the London skyline. Xander caught his breath as the hazy golden light illuminated his handsome face. It reflected in his green eyes as he looked out over the city with something like wonder.

"I keep expecting to wake up from this dream any minute," he said, his voice suspiciously hoarse.

TWENTY-THREE

Xander tore his eyes away from Manisha's earnest face to gaze out across the city he'd called home for far more than a lifetime. Sunlight spilled over the glittering skyscrapers clustered on the banks of the Thames and illuminated the historic buildings around Trafalgar Square, bringing cold glass and stone to life with a soft yellow-orange glow.

How pathetically symbolic it all seemed right now. Christ, look at him. He was in danger of turning into some second-rate Lord Byron, waxing lyrical over the sunrise.

But still, as it touched his deathly pale face with a warm caress, his eyes burned and prickled in a way that had nothing to do with vampire vulnerabilities to daylight. How was it conceivable that he was standing here with his hands wrapped around his soulmate's arms, looking out across the city at dawn?

The problem with things that were too good to be true was that they were generally too good to be true. As soon as you let your guard down and accepted them, something came along to pull the rug out from beneath your feet and dump you straight onto your arse. He'd learned that lesson a long, long time ago on what had turned out to be the worst night of his life.

Manisha was watching him watch the sun, but now she cocked her head at him. Of course, he realized. His shields had been utter shite since he'd awoken chained to a bike rack with werewolf blood running through his veins, so she had probably just heard every last word of his silent musings.

This was confirmed a moment later when she said, "Isn't it better to enjoy the good things while you have them, rather than spend a lifetime frozen in place, worrying that the rug will disappear?"

He looked down at her again, drinking in her beautiful features with the same intense gaze he'd spared earlier for the sunlit city behind her.

"I'm afraid I really wouldn't know," he said. After all, he'd devoted all his spare time and energy chasing fleeting oblivion—the very opposite of living in the moment. In fact, he was reasonably certain that he hadn't spent this much time focusing on strong emotions without fleeing into a chemical haze since the night a demon had torn his soul apart.

Predictably, the thought that came immediately on the heels of that one was, *Christ, I need a drink.*

"Yeah," Manisha said with a wan smile that reminded him just exactly how much she'd gone through in the past few weeks. "You know what? I think drinking right now is a plan I can get behind."

Berating himself for letting his admittedly numerous and deep-seated issues distract him from what *she* needed, he took a deep breath and tried to lighten the mood.

"God help me," he said. "I've just realized that I'll have to stop feeding from alcoholics and drug addicts now, since they can't give meaningful consent. I may need to rethink this entire plan."

She turned in his arms, facing him properly now with her back to the wall of the terrace. "So, you did a lot of that kind of thing before, I take it?"

He snorted. "You could say that. Though as coping mechanisms go, it's a fairly ineffectual one for a vampire, I'm sorry to say. Drugs barely work, and have no long-term effects at all. Which is probably just as well, since I really *wouldn't* have any brain cells left otherwise. Or, you know, a liver."

Looking back, he thought that perhaps the ritual involved in finding an appropriate victim and obtaining their blood had become as much a part of the distraction from his shitty life as the few minutes of resulting buzz. She nodded in understanding.

"But it does help for a little bit?" she asked, and that haunted look was still very much present behind her deep brown eyes.

He shook his head slowly. "I'm not sure how to answer that. I'm still here, and I haven't snapped completely. I suppose it must have done."

She pressed her hand flat against his chest. It was the same gesture she had used earlier in the bedroom, when she'd broken through his mental shields as though they were made of spun glass. He let her walk him backwards, maneuvering him around the table and chairs until the backs of his knees hit the edge of the chaise lounge. Another push, and he toppled into it, looking up at her five-foot-three-inch frame and feeling something start to unravel inside him.

"Stay here," she said, and disappeared into the flat. She emerged a few moments later, examining a bottle of *Sauvignon Blanc* held in her hands. "Since it wasn't refrigerated, can I safely assume this is wine and not plasma? Despite the super-classy screw-top?"

He looked at her curiously. "The wine rack is for guests. It's certified plasma-free, I promise. And it's a common misconception that all good-quality wine uses corks. Those meant to be drunk young often benefit from the airtight seal of a screw top. It helps keep them crisp."

She quirked a brow in acknowledgement. "Huh. Well… live and learn, I guess." She twisted the cap off and sniffed at the contents. "Right — give me a minute, here. It's been a while."

Xander watched in mild shock as she tipped the bottle back, her throat working as she swallowed. Perhaps it shouldn't be so surprising, since she still craved solid food as well as blood. But there were other considerations beyond the mere fact of her being able to swallow the stuff without it coming right back up.

"And here I had you pegged as a good little Buddhist girl," he said, trying not to focus too closely on the movement of her throat muscles and what it was doing to his libido.

She lowered the bottle, now about a quarter of the way drained. "You know, some advanced Vajrayana practitioners consider alcohol a valuable tool for assisting in the divestment of the ego," she said solemnly.

"And are you an advanced Vajrayana practitioner?" he asked.

At that, she huffed a breath of harsh laughter. "Uh... *no*. Not even close. Of course, I haven't always been a good little Buddhist girl, either. Between my periodic overindulgence in alcohol and my occasional trysts with boys as a teenager, I'm sure my parents frequently despaired of me."

"Shocking," Xander said in a gently teasing tone, even as the revelation of Manisha's minor bouts of adolescent rebellion made an almost overwhelming ache of fondness surge inside him.

She knocked back another few swallows of the wine and wiped a forearm across her mouth, the movement delightfully unguarded as she paced along the wall of the terrace, looking out over the city.

"They're gone now," she said quietly. "My parents, I mean. And I never had any brothers or sisters, so there's really no one left to disapprove, I suppose." She gave a harsh little snort of bitter amusement. "I think everyone assumes that I ended up as part of Sangye's retinue because I'm some sort of extra-devout, holier-than-thou Buddhist paragon. But, actually, it was because they needed a housekeeper when they arrived in India, I was looking for work at the time, and Jampa and I hit it off."

"Manisha..." he said quietly, feeling the fresh swell of distress building within her mind at the reminder of Sangye and his mother.

She threw the wine back again, swallowing several times, and when she lowered it her voice grew tight. "No one ever thought I'd end up being Sangye's last line of protection. Though if they had, they probably wouldn't have been surprised that I failed at it so spectacularly."

"*Manisha.*" He put more force behind the word that time, and she paused in her pacing, not looking at him as he continued. "We're not giving up on them, you know. Not on Sangye; not on Snag."

What started as a nod became a shake of the head, the sentiment behind it caught somewhere between agreement and disagreement. "I... I know. I know you'll try to find him. Them."

"Of course we will." He fought the urge to go to her, sensing that it was important to let her come to him instead. Though, that sort of psychological give and take was probably much subtler when the person you were with couldn't pluck thoughts straight out of your mind.

She shot him a faintly sheepish glance, the first hint of alcohol-fog becoming visible in her eyes, though her words were still clear and precise.

"Sorry. I guess I was trying to give you a chance to make your escape without it turning into a big drama," she said. "Because my wolf is on edge and I really, really need a break from thinking right now. So, if you're still here when this bottle is finished... well, things are probably going to degenerate into a repeat of the freezer incident."

... and just like that, Xander was hard as a fucking rock.

"Bloody Christ, Manisha. You don't need to finish the bottle if that's your end game. *Come here.*"

She looked immediately reassured, as if she were honestly still hung up on her perceived 'sexual assault of an unwilling vampire' from the other night. Still, she shook her head. "No, wine first. You didn't see how much alcohol the other werewolves could pack away." Her eyes burned into his, golden light kindling in their depths. "Believe me, if this bottle is going to serve two, we'll need all of it."

A noise rumbled up from his chest, the unfamiliar new presence of the wolf inside him rising and stretching in anticipation. "Oh, yes?" His voice went low and rough. "In that case, get your arse over here and you can finish it while I get that robe untied."

A wild, untethered look came over her face, her eyes flaring brilliantly. Xander knew his own matched them, burning green as his fangs pressed into the sides of his cheeks. To his utter relief, she walked over to him without hesitation and sank down, straddling him as he leaned back against the chaise lounge.

He reached along the bond, wanting his own reassurance that this was truly Manisha talking and not the booze. Her mind remained sharp and bright, the wine barely beginning to touch her control.

Told you. It's a werewolf thing, apparently, she said, and he couldn't stop the lazy smile that pulled one corner his lips back, revealing a hint of fang.

So you did, he returned. *But I'm sure you understand why I wanted to see for myself.*

"Yeah," she breathed. "Yeah, I get it." With that, she closed her eyes, and let him see *everything*.

Her memories of the distant past, of the love they'd shared before tragedy struck. Her utter relief at not being alone after the massacre at the warehouse. Her gratitude for his comfort and protection in bringing her back to his home to care for her when she was on the verge of physical and emotional collapse. How it had felt to drink his blood, and the jolt she'd felt upon realizing that not only wasn't he disgusted—he was taking pleasure from it. The blanket of warm contentment that had settled over her when he convinced her to shift form with him, and watched over her while she curled up to sleep as the wolf.

How every precious, fleeting moment of respite she'd experienced since escaping the werewolves had taken place in his embrace.

Right now, Xander wanted to wrap her up in his arms and never let go. He wanted to deliver Sangye to her unharmed, and spirit both of them away to some magical place where Bael could never touch them again. He wanted to drink from her veins. He wanted to feed their mingled blood right back to her, and fuck her until neither one of them could remember their own names.

Yes, she thought, sounding young and unguarded. *I want all that. I want to forget. Please… can't we both just forget for a little while?*

"Manisha, love," he said, cupping her cheek in his hand. "I am the world's foremost expert on forgetting for a little while. Now—why don't you get back to drinking, and we'll go on from there."

She did, and he immediately turned his attention toward doing everything in his power to distract her. Happily for him, she still wore only the terrycloth robe he'd draped around her after waking her earlier to speak to the others. Xander hooked a finger in the fold covering her left breast and drew it slowly to the side, his fingertip brushing along the olive-toned skin that was revealed, inch by inch.

Manisha wanted to forget, and Xander found that he wanted nothing more than to give her whatever she desired. If that meant giving himself permission for a few hours not to obsess over the darkness that surrounded them... if it meant not questioning how he had somehow gone from being a miserable sod to the luckiest man alive... well, so be it. She wasn't the only one who needed to set down the heavy weight on her shoulders for a bit.

Manisha went still as his finger trailed over the swell of her breast, a soft noise emerging from her lips. When the smooth globe was revealed in its entirety, she muttered something in Hindi and threw back the bottle, chugging the remaining contents without ceremony. Xander's smile grew wider as he allowed all the other problems swirling around them to fall away.

"Better now?" he asked, feeling through the bond as Manisha's muscles finally began to relax, the wine smoothing away some of the sharp edges of her thoughts. It probably wouldn't last any longer for her than it ever did for him, but he fully intended them both to be distracted for other reasons by the time it wore off.

"Promises, promises," she breathed, melting into him a little further. The bottle clattered to the terrace floor, glass ringing as it rolled a short distance and fetched up against a random piece of furniture.

TWENTY-FOUR

Xander closed his fingers around one end of the belt holding the robe shut at her waist and tugged, loosening the knot until the soft garment fell open, revealing more dusky flesh.

"One more thing," he told her in a low voice. "This is not, in fact, going to be a repeat of the so-called *freezer incident*. If you think I'm going to be done with you in mere minutes when we have *hours* to ourselves, then—closet 'bad girl' or not—you lack imagination."

She shivered against him, the tiny movement sending an answering frisson up his spine.

"I can't help noticing you're still sober," she said. "Why is that? I didn't chug an entire bottle of screw-top wine for my health, you know."

Good god. Could this woman be any more perfect?

A brief brush of thoughts confirmed that she was well aware of what she was offering, and also revealed a tangle of confused memories from the night of the full moon—his fangs sinking into her neck; the explosion of pleasure-pain that drove the wolf wild. That need to be held in place and marked by her mate, combined now with the newly risen vampire instinct to revel in blood.

Nature, red in tooth and claw? he thought. *Christ, Manisha, you're killing me, here.*

Bending her backwards, he dipped his head and caught a dusky nipple between his teeth, letting his fangs scrape along the tender skin around her areola without piercing it. Her flesh tasted as succulent as he'd known it would, and he marveled now that he'd ever found the smell of werewolf anything other than intoxicating.

Her head fell back and she groaned, the sound rushing straight to his cock. Xander sucked on the pebbled point, more of his control falling by the wayside as she arched, trying to press her breast harder against his mouth. The point of one fang slipped into delicate skin, a drop of blood welling up.

The taste exploded across his tongue, and even without the wine she'd drunk, it would have been pure ambrosia. He drew harder on her breast, not deepening the tiny puncture, but instead reveling in the slow tease of her blood squeezing out a droplet at a time. She let out a weak cry, her palms splayed against his chest. When he scraped a fingernail across the painfully hard point of her other nipple, her fingers curled into claws. The half-moons of her nails pricked his skin through the fabric of his shirt, waking every nerve.

His cock was trapped between them, and he hummed around her breast when she rolled her hips, trying to get friction. Xander let go of her nipple, ignoring her moan of disappointment as he lapped at the little dribble of blood that trickled down from the puncture he'd left.

It didn't heal immediately, making him cognizant of the fact that vampire and werewolf blood still interfered with each other in some ways. And while he had absolutely no problem with ending up covered in bites and claw marks at the end of this, he didn't want her to end up a bloody mess of wounds as well... even if that little sluggishly bleeding smear of red on her chest *was* driving him slowly insane.

Sometimes, he decided, the old clichés were still the best. With that in mind, he kissed his way up from her nipple to her collarbone, lifting one of his hands to tangle in the thick, waist-length hair he couldn't seem to get enough of, and lowered his other hand to cup her thigh. The grip allowed him to ease her up from his lap until she was no longer rutting on him—and, more importantly, until he could get his fingertips against the slick heat of her center.

Jesus, Manisha, you're soaked, he observed silently, teasing her wet folds with light strokes up and down her length. Meanwhile, he nibbled his way up her throat, pausing over a thrumming vein that smelled and tasted like paradise. He let his fingers explore her sex while his lips and tongue explored the side of her neck, searching out the perfect place to strike.

She shuddered, trying to press onto both his fingers and his fangs at the same time. He kept both touches light, right up until the moment her grasping fingers clenched at his shirt and yanked it apart, popping buttons loose as she tore it open.

Well, all right, then, he thought. Though, in her defense, sometimes teasing really was overrated.

With a low hiss of warning, he dragged her head to the side and sank his fangs into her neck at the same moment he thrust two fingers inside her sex, pressing in to the third knuckle. Alcohol-infused blood flowed into his mouth, and tight heat clamped around his fingers. Manisha gasped raggedly, her hands tangling in the fabric of his abused shirt. Xander swallowed the heady liquid gushing over his tongue, feeling the feedback loop of their mental connection swell under the sensations they were both experiencing.

He stroked her pulsing inner walls, pulling out to circle her clit with slick fingertips before thrusting in again, reveling in the sensations coming through the bond. He tried to send back the exquisite feeling of her blood slipping down his throat; their life forces mingling.

Only when her dizzy climb reached its summit and left her poised on the edge of release did he drag up his battered mental shields, not wanting to spend in his trousers like a virgin the moment her climax hit. Even so, his cock twitched and throbbed almost painfully when her body went rigid, her walls fluttering around his fingers. He coaxed her through the orgasm, drawing things out as long as he could.

The flow of blood from her neck was slowing now, even as the alcohol in it started to hit him, quieting the endless confusion of circling thoughts that plagued him so much of the time. He pulled away from her throat and stilled his fingers inside her, enjoying the last weak quivers as her muscles worked around him.

She sagged into his embrace, and he steadied her, soaking up the boneless feeling of contentment flowing along the bond, mixing and merging with the buzz of blood and wine. Apparently, this was an effective way to spare his trouser fly the same tragic end his shirt had suffered, because rather than ripping it open, she fumbled at the closures with clumsy fingers.

"Need you," she murmured against his neck, making the fine hairs on his nape stand at attention. "Need more... need all of you..."

He slipped his fingers out of her warm depths and helped her get the damned trousers out of the way, lifting his hips enough to slide them down and free his cock without dislodging her from his lap.

Taking a bare instant to be thankful that he didn't generally bother with underwear, he lifted her hips and impaled her on his aching cock. Just as it had the morning after the full moon, the simple act of sliding into her body slotted something in his life into place, making him feel whole in a way he had never thought to experience again after the agony of his soul being rent in two.

Physical pleasure was a dim flicker of candlelight compared to the blazing bonfire of reunion with his soul's true mate.

Oh, yes. Her mental words were a sigh of relief. *Finally...*

They didn't even move. They just lay there, sprawled on the chaise lounge with her legs wrapped around him, and his arms wrapped around her.

"*Manisha*," he breathed.

As he had suspected might be the case after he'd drunk so deeply from her, he felt her hunger begin to grow through the link. It started as a feeling of emptiness low in her belly that tangled with her banked sexual desire and grew into an ache. With his cock surrounded by her heat and her lips brushing the half-healed bite on his neck from her first feeding in the shower, the anticipation of what was to come was as much pleasure as agony.

He didn't try to rush her, instead rolling his head back to bare his throat to her as her lips and teeth toyed with the tender wound. Then and there, he decided that, as long as being some kind of fucked-up vampire/werewolf hybrid meant he could wear the marks of her fangs on his body for the rest of eternity, it was bloody well worth it.

Eventually, her hunger overcame her drowsy, post-orgasmic lassitude, and sharp teeth sank into his ravaged flesh. His hips jerked deeper into her of their own accord, and all thoughts of a lazy, hours-long shag flew away into the London morning. She ground against his lap and swallowed him down, taking back the blood he'd pulled from her earlier, and then some.

Her feeding was messy and wild—he could feel his blood dribbling down in ribbons from the place where her lips were fastened around his throat. Any human unlucky enough to stumble upon the scene would doubtless have been horrified. The two of them writhed together, Xander arching up to meet her thrusts while their upper bodies slid together, slick with blood. He managed to worm a hand in between them so he could palm the breast he'd nicked earlier, red staining his fingers as he pinched and plucked at her nipple.

He'd been absolutely right the first time she'd fed from him — the lightheaded feeling as she drained him really was sublime with his cock buried inside her.

"It's all yours," he said, eyes open and staring at the white clouds and blue sky above as the sun shone down on them. "Take all of it... all of me..."

In what seemed like no time at all, her movements grew desperate and her walls clamped around him. Release coiled hot and insistent at the base of his spine, exploding outward when she grunted against the abused skin of his throat and clamped her jaws into him *hard*.

Coming with her while his mental shields were down was almost too much — the London sky went hazy and dark, his brain losing the metaphorical arm-wrestling match over the remaining blood in his body to his pulsing prick.

Which only went to show that his body, at least, had its priorities firmly in the right place.

The feeling of fangs retracting from his neck brought him back to a modicum of awareness some unknown amount of time later. Manisha was a soft, sleepy weight against him. A low, pleasant hum like white noise suffused the bond, empty of everything except sexual afterglow.

The decision whether or not to move seemed to take on a deeply significant weight, and Xander eventually compromised by swinging his legs up so he was lying full-length along the chaise with

Manisha draped over him like a blanket. She murmured some sort of wordless, approving noise and settled herself a little more fully onto him.

For the first time in longer than he cared to remember, Xander took a deep breath and slipped into a contented doze, without a single thought for anything but the present moment.

TWENTY-FIVE

Manisha awoke slowly to the feeling of rhyth-
mic swaying. She curled into the strong arms
holding her, and realized with drowsy curiosity
that she was being carried bridal-style.

"Mmm… Xander?" she asked sleepily. "Wha's
happening?"

Lips brushed her forehead. "A shower, followed by bed, I should think. How are you?"

She took stock. *Good,* she decided. *Don't want
to have to face everything yet.*

*All you're facing right now is a spray of warm wa-
ter,* he sent back. A mental curl of amusement
brushed at her awareness. *Come now… did I say I
was done with you yet?*

A lazy flush of desire rose from her belly despite what they'd done earlier. She relaxed, letting
the wolf have control again. Content to set aside
human concerns for a few more hours, or however
long they had left before reality once more intruded. In the meantime, this fantasy world of luxury
and sex would do… just fine.

Xander set her on her feet on the heated tile
floor of the master bathroom. She let her robe slide
down her arms, feeling dried blood flake on her
skin. Xander busied himself running the water to
just the right temperature, and she busied herself

by coming up behind him and easing the shirt off his shoulders.

He let his arms drop so she could get it off, then he turned to face her. Still letting the wolf lead, she licked a stripe along the trail of mostly dried blood leading down from his throat to his chest, while her hands unfastened his trousers and slid them down. They pooled on the floor, and he stepped out of them.

He was well built without being muscle bound, she realized—beautifully proportioned with a smooth, hairless chest and defined arms and legs. His skin was strikingly pale even after the time they'd spent in the morning sun. She realized with a possessive lurch that his pallor was probably due to the fact that a good portion of his blood was currently running in her veins, not his.

"Finally got you properly naked," she said, looking him up and down with satisfaction, noting that blood loss hadn't stopped his erection from rising to half-mast already. "It took long enough."

A smile twitched at one corner of his mouth. "The wolf was naked last night. Don't be species-ist."

She tried to smile back, but even now, outside pressures were starting to swirl back in as she woke up properly.

"Oh, no," he said, opening the door and ushering her into the familiar steamy shower. "None of that, now. Soap. Shampoo. Cunnilingus. More shagging. Sleep."

That shocked a short laugh from her. "Bit sure of yourself, aren't you?" she asked, as he crowded her up against the wall.

"Not in the least," he replied easily. "I'm still expecting to wake up from this any minute, love. Which is all the more reason to take advantage while I can."

He poured soap into his hands, forgoing a washcloth in favor of sliding his palms over her upper body directly, lathering her shoulders, arms, and breasts with firm strokes. Manisha let her head fall back against the glass, relief flooding her as her mind once again went warm, pliant, and empty.

As it had the first time he'd brought her in here to wash the blood from her body, the sudsy water ran rusty for a few moments before growing clear. The tiny puncture on her breast was scabbed over, though it hadn't disappeared yet. The bite mark on her neck was still tender, and he washed around the edges carefully.

Apparently, however, being a werewolf and/or vampire was giving her a kink for pain, because the sting of soap against the fang marks drew a high-pitched whine from her throat, which tailed into a needy moan.

Xander breathed out sharply in response, his hands going still. "You know what? Fuck shampoo. Shampoo is vastly overrated."

And then he was crashing to his knees in front of her, dragging one of her legs over his shoulder and steadying her with a rock-solid grip on her hip to keep her upright. A moment later, his mouth was on her sex, and no teenage tryst with an awkward, fumbling boy had *ever* prepared her for this.

I should fucking well hope not, he sent along the link, his mental voice a growl. Manisha squeezed her eyes shut and panted. Hot water pelted her, running in rivulets down her body to the place where a cool tongue and sharp teeth methodically shattered her into a million pieces.

-o-o-o-

Xander made good on his promise to make her forget everything for a few hours. They had sex on the bed. They had sex in the kitchen. They had sex in the jetted Japanese soaking tub. They shifted into wolf form and had rough and dirty animal sex on his expensive Turkish rug... at which point Manisha discovered what knotting was and why it was basically the best thing ever.

By the time Xander finally tucked her against his side in the massive bed and pulled the elegant black and gray comforter over them, Manisha was one huge swirling muddle of happy, exhausted endorphins, and she slept the sleep of the dead — or should that be the *undead*? — for hours.

She awoke to find herself still wrapped around Xander, who was propped up against a pile of pillows drinking one-handed from a bottle of blood while she drooled all over his opposite shoulder.

"Evening, love," he greeted, and offered her the bottle once she'd peeled herself off of him enough to roll up on an elbow. "Breakfast?"

She took the bottle and drank from it, noticing on the first swallow that she was developing a decided preference for Xander's blood over bottled blood. She also noticed that while she was definitely hungry, it wasn't the same sort of mindless animal hunger she'd felt the last few times.

"You're already getting stronger," he said, presumably in response to her mental observations. "Gaining control."

"Hmm," she replied, not really up to much more conversation. Was blood going to be her new coffee now? The kick she needed before she could face the day or hold an intelligent conversation?

She drank some more and offered it back, but Xander waved her off, indicating he'd had enough. Shrugging, she tipped it up and let the last few swallows slide down her throat. When she was done, he took the empty bottle and stretched over to set it on the bedside table. When his green eyes returned to her, there was a hint of wariness behind them.

"Just to be perfectly clear and aboveboard, is this going to be the point when you realize what you've done and run screaming for the hills?" he asked.

She blinked at him. "Why?" she asked cautiously. "Are you hoping I will so it saves you having to do it? I get that it could be awkward since this is, you know, *your flat* and everything."

The tension ran out of his shoulders and he flopped back down, drawing her with him until she was once more curled up with her head on his shoulder.

"No," he said. "No, I definitely wasn't hoping for that."

It wasn't yet second nature for her to look inward and feel what was running through his mind, but it occurred to her once he'd spoken. Indeed, his relief across the bond was palpable.

"Okay, good," she said. "I've got nowhere to run and it's just about the last thing I want to do right now anyway." She swallowed. "This really is kind of awkward, isn't it?"

His hand came up to cradle the back of her head, stroking her scalp in a way that made her want to slide right back down into sleep. "I think it will stop being awkward if we can both accept that even though we're a mess, we'll be less of a mess if we face things together."

The tidal wave of relief that swamped her at the idea of letting herself become part of this bizarre vampire family of his took her by surprise. "I'd like that," she said, choking a bit on the words.

"Oh, thank god," he said in a rush, his voice a bit hoarse as well. He cleared his throat. "Well, then. The others will probably show up in an hour or so, and we'll plan our next move properly now that everyone has had a chance to rest."

She nodded. "Does that mean there's time for a quickie in the shower first?"

His huff of laughter was silent, but she felt his chest move beneath her cheek.

"Fucking hell, Manisha. If this is what positive karma looks like, I must have accumulated it when I was either too drunk or too stoned to remember afterward what good deeds I'd performed." He stroked a strand of hair back from her face and hooked it over her ear. "I expect there's time. And if there's not, the others will just have to wait on us. It's not as though I haven't been subjected to their near-constant shagging over the past few months. Turnabout, and all that."

She rolled into a sitting position, letting the sheets slide down. "Tomorrow, I want to try to contact my relatives in Swansea. Will you come, in case things go badly and I need to make them forget?"

His fingertips trailed over the tender place on her neck where his fangs had pierced her earlier. "Try to keep me away."

She smiled as he rolled onto an elbow, facing her.

"I should also talk to a few of my people privately about blood," he continued. "People from the company who I think we can trust. Starting with the pimply kid down in the IT department who's a conspiracy theorist. I bet he'll lap this story up with a spoon. I'd… like you to come with me for that, as well."

She smiled, the expression feeling genuine for the first time in days, if not weeks. "Do I look like someone who would miss the chance for a tour of a vampire-owned solar panel company?"

The corners of his eyes crinkled. "You look… *beautiful*. That's how you look. Now come on, love—stop being a layabout. There's a shower through that door with our names on it, and we'll have guests to scandalize before long."

EPILOGUE

(A silent conversation in the dark.)

Why did you surrender yourself to the demon, Elder?

Silence.

He'll destroy you.

Perhaps, child.

I'm so hungry. It aches…

Then feed.

But I don't want to.

You must.

Why? Why Must I?

For strength.

What about your strength?

Silence.

Elder? What about your strength?

My strength does not lie here. It resides elsewhere. When the time is right, I will have whatever strength I require.

Are you sure?

I am sure.

Rustling. Glowing eyes in the dark.

Yes. That's better. Feed now, child. Don't concern your-self with me.

finis

The *Circle of Blood* series continues in *Book Five: Lover's Atonement.*

To get the free prequel to the *Circle of Blood* series sent directly to your inbox, visit www.rasteffan.com/circle

Printed in Great Britain
by Amazon